the Natural Genius of Ants

Also by Betty Culley

Down to Earth

the Natural Genius of Ants

BETTY CULLEY

Crown Books for Young Readers

New York

Text copyright © 2022 by Betty Culley
Jacket art and interior illustrations copyright © 2022 by The Brave Union

All rights reserved. Published in the United States by Crown Books for Young Readers, an imprint of Random House Children's Books, a division of Penguin Random House LLC, New York.

Crown and the colophon are registered trademarks of Penguin Random House LLC.

Visit us on the Web! rhcbooks.com

Educators and librarians, for a variety of teaching tools, visit us at RHTeachersLibrarians.com

Library of Congress Cataloging-in-Publication Data is available upon request.
ISBN 978-0-593-17577-4 (hardcover) — ISBN 978-0-593-17579-8 (ebk)

The text of this book is set in 11.5-point Bell MT Pro.
Interior design by Andrea Lau

Printed in the United States of America
10 9 8 7 6 5 4 3 2 1
First Edition

To Denis, for everything

ONE

The Mistake

Dad said being in Kettle Hole was like going back in time, but I didn't know what he meant until we got here. The trees are tall and straight, and farm fields stretch out to the sky. There are gigantic bullfrogs with eyes as big as nickels, and trucks filled with logs rumble down the dirt roads, blowing up dust. Instead of streetlights shining outside our windows, we're in a place so dark at night you feel invisible. A place where you hear coyotes howl and yip. Dad says they live deep in the woods, even though it sounds like they're very close.

We came here because of my father's mistake. He can't forgive himself for what he did. It doesn't matter that he's a doctor, and doctors make mistakes like everybody else.

After the baby died, Mom tried to explain why Dad was so sad. She said people are human and she'd gotten things wrong at work, too.

"Did any parasites die?" I asked. She's studying a parasite that makes people lose their vision. It's so small you can only see it through a special microscope.

My little brother Roger's eyes got very big.

Since Dad's mistake, my mouth has been on autopilot.

"Harvard!" Mom said my name once, like a warning, and quickly looked around to see if Dad had heard me. Luckily, he hadn't.

For five months after his mistake, Dad didn't work. He didn't leave our apartment on the fifth floor except to get a haircut. He cried when no one was looking and even when everyone was looking.

Then he got the idea for us to go to Kettle Hole for the summer, the place where he grew up. His childhood friend Vernon Knowles was renting out his house six states away from our apartment and the hospital where Dad used to work.

"You know I can't leave my research right now," Mom said when Dad told us about his plan.

"I know you can't leave the parasites. They *need* you so much. They *depend* on you. They can't *live* without you," I said. Mom and I collect parasite jokes.

Later, I overheard Mom and Dad talking in their bedroom. She asked him why he wanted to go to Kettle Hole. In his thought-out, list-making way, he gave her three reasons.

"People know me as the Corson boy there, not Dr. Corson. Kettle Hole is always in my heart, even though I haven't been back since my grandfather's funeral. And Robert Frost was right—that home is the place where, when you have to go there, they have to take you in."

Mom had one answer to his three reasons.

"If that's what you need to do, Marshall."

Dad answered back, "Vern thought Earlene would make it, but she's been gone six months and he's in a spot trying to pay off her medical bills and raise his daughter. He was going to lose the house, and we need a place to stay. Give me this time with the boys, Dee. Maybe I can do something right and make it a summer they will always remember."

It was quiet then, and I peeked into their room. Mom had her arms around Dad, her cheek pressed against his. He just stood there with his arms hanging down, like he didn't have enough energy to hug her back.

Mom answered, "You were born to be a doctor, Marshall. Please use this summer to figure out a way to forgive yourself."

To get to Kettle Hole, we drove east for more than a day and then headed north. The highway in Maine was only two lanes, and the farther north we went the less cars there were on the road.

I've never been to the town where my father grew up. Mom grew up in the city where we live, but Mom's mother, my abuela, is from the Dominican Republic. I've never been there, either. Part of the year she lives right near us, and part of the year she goes back to the DR to see family.

"The fields and the woods are just how I remember," Dad said when we got off the highway. "It's like going back in time."

"Then you better speed up," I blurted out.

Dad drove exactly five miles under the speed limit, both hands on the wheel.

"Why would I want to do that?" he asked without turning his head away from the road.

"So we get there before you're too young to drive. And I'm only ten, so if you go too slow, I'll disappear."

I saw a little smile on Dad's face in the rearview mirror, but he didn't drive any faster.

Being on a long car trip makes you think about things.

Roger, I know, thought about one thing. The food in the cooler on the back seat between us. He'd watched Dad fill it and he had a contest with himself to eat some of everything packed in there. Grapes, cheese slices, juice boxes, macaroni and cheese, oatmeal raisin cookies.

Mom wouldn't have let Roger eat so much, but Dad was busy driving. And when Roger had food in his mouth, he wasn't asking the same thing over and over—*What do you think Mommy is doing RIGHT NOW?* Or saying, *If Mommy was here, she'd sing the car song.* I have no idea what the car song is, but Roger sang the only lines he remembered until they were stamped in my brain.

Car, car, car

Far, far, far

While Roger ate, I looked out my window and thought about the things people say about mistakes, all of which are wrong:

Mistakes happen.

Don't be afraid to make mistakes.

It's only a mistake.

You learn from your mistakes.

Don't worry. It was an honest mistake.

None of those things are true, I thought, because if they were, Dad would still be taking care of the smallest and sickest babies in the hospital instead of planning our summer to remember. Roger wouldn't be one state away from a bellyache after eating his hundredth snack. All I could do, as we got closer and closer to Kettle Hole, was hope that going back to the place where Dad grew up wouldn't turn out to be another mistake.

TWO

One Word or Two?

When we finally pull up in front of Mr. Knowles's house in Kettle Hole, it's dark all around us, with only one light shining on a porch the whole length of the house. Dad shuts off the motor and opens the car door. Roger snores in his sleep.

"Listen," Dad says. "Barred owls."

There's an eerie hooting noise and then cries like monkeys screaming. Dad stands there looking into the woods where the sounds are coming from.

"Do you have the key to the house?" I ask.

"It should be open," he says.

That's how I end up being the first one in, carrying my backpack over my shoulder. I feel for a switch on the wall, and the room lights up. The floor is wood and the house smells like the cabin I stayed in at summer camp last year. It's colder inside the house than outside. The living room has a couch and chair at one end and a desk and floor lamp in a corner. There's a kitchen with a square table and four chairs. The windows are low and tall, and none of them have curtains.

Up a set of stairs are three bedrooms and a bathroom. One bedroom has a big bed like Mom and Dad's. I drop my backpack on the bed in the smaller of the other two. This way there's no tears from Roger for getting *the worst room*. Plus the smallest room has a window that looks out onto a roof, and a long closet under a sloping wall. That night I fall asleep on the bed in the room without even taking my sneakers off.

The morning after we arrive, I'm the last one awake. Dad is in the kitchen and I smell his coffee brewing. Roger is at the kitchen table.

"What are Roger and I going to do here?" I ask Dad.

"Any number of things," he says. "See what catches your eye, where your interests take you."

Dad's face is pale from spending the past five months inside, his eyelashes almost see-through, and his hair is the same light brown as Roger's, but thinner on top.

"What about you? What are *you* going to do?" I ask him.

"I'm going to work on being a better parent," he says.

"Better how? Who are you competing against?" The words are out before I have a chance to think.

Dad answers in a serious voice.

"Better in all ways, Harvard. More involved. More focused. More adaptable."

"You're hired. When can you start?"

Dad ignores or doesn't notice that I'm being mouthy. He drops toast on plates, puts out jelly, shakes the orange juice container, and spins silverware across the table so it lands exactly in front of where we're each sitting. Then he sits down and clasps his hands on the table in front of himself.

He's wearing a white short-sleeved button-down shirt, and in the front pocket there's a pen and a mini notepad.

"I didn't bring the computer because there's no internet connection in the house. It's also hard for me to get reception on my cell phone unless I'm outside. But anytime you want to call Mom you can use the house phone there on the desk."

"Is that what you meant by going back in time?" I ask.

"Internet access and TV cost money Vern doesn't have. I think you'll find plenty of things to keep you busy here. Also, I want you both to know you can talk to me about anything, and ask whatever questions you have."

I can't stop myself. "Which came first, the chicken or the egg?"

"Which came first, the chicken or the egg?" Roger repeats, tipping himself out of his chair and onto the kitchen floor laughing. He's still holding a piece of jelly toast in one hand.

Roger is five and falls on the floor whenever he thinks something is really funny.

"Roger, back in your chair," Dad says automatically.

"That's an eternal question, isn't it? I don't have an answer. I also wanted you to know you can invite your friends here anytime. If they fly up, we can meet them at the airport."

There's only my friend Tobias who I'd want to come. He's the friend who never asked why Dad was always home or why Dad would sometimes cover his eyes with his hands and turn away. Tobias would sit at the kitchen island while Dad was cooking or cleaning up and tell him stories about what happened at school.

"The word *vacationland*. Would you think it was one word or two?" I ask.

On the drive here I saw the Maine license plates, white with black letters and the word *vacationland* on the bottom.

"I don't know. Probably two?" Dad guesses.

"That's what I thought, but it was one word on the Maine license plates. *Vacationland*. Not *vacation land*. It doesn't make sense."

I don't stop there.

"It's hard to know, right? Like why is *toothbrush* one word but *swimming pool* is two words?"

"Swimming pool. Can we get a swimming pool?" Roger asks.

"And *bathroom* and *spaceship* are one word, but *ice cream* is two words."

"That *is* a puzzle," Dad says, looking at his plate. He cuts the crusts off his toast with a knife and fork, cuts the toast into four squares, then cuts the squares into perfect triangles.

"I want ice cream, too. Swimming pool. Bathroom.

Spaceship. Swimming pool. Bathroom. Spaceship. Ice cream," Roger says over and over, because whatever I say, Roger wants to say at least twice.

Dad puts down his knife and fork. He presses his hand on his throat, over the place where his stethoscope used to hang. When I first started blurting things out, Mom said, *If you can, Harvard, before you say something you might regret or that could hurt someone's feelings, ask yourself why you're saying it. And if you know the reason and it's a good reason, then go ahead.*

But the sadder Dad is, the more I can't stop to ask myself anything. Or maybe I don't try because what if some of those words make him laugh again?

THREE

Heat Lightning

On our first day in Kettle Hole, I see a bull-
frog and a skinny snake with yellow stripes in the
woods, and get bitten by bugs Dad calls deerflies. Roger
plays ball with Dad, climbs in the tire swing that's hanging
from a tree, and rocks himself in a hammock on the back
lawn.

Dad says Vernon Knowles and his daughter are supposed
to stop by around dark. I'm near the open window when a
man and a girl walk up the stone step onto the porch. The
sun hangs right over the tops of the trees, and the sky is
orange and pink.

The porch light shines on them. The man is wearing a
T-shirt and jeans.

"I don't think I've ever knocked on this door before," he says.

The girl leans against him. He puts his arm around her. The girl's face reminds me of a bird. It's triangle-shaped, with her chin the bottom point and her brown eyes far apart above a small sharp nose. Her brown hair hangs down past her shoulders.

"Me neither," she says.

"They're here," I call to Dad, "but they're just standing there on the porch."

Dad rushes to the door and opens it wide. The man comes in first. He's shorter than Dad and his arms are thick and muscly, like a weight lifter's. His hair is almost as dark as mine and Mom's.

Dad hugs the man, who thumps him on the back.

"Marshall Corson, Spelling Bee King of Kettle Hole," his friend says. "Welcome back!"

"Vern," Dad says. "It's been too long."

Mr. Knowles squeezes Dad's shoulder.

"Thank you, Marshall, for helping me keep my promise to Earlene and stopping us from losing the house. I'm sure my father is looking down on me, shaking his fist that I took out a second mortgage on the homestead."

"No, it's you, Vern, who helped me, more than you know. Boys," Dad says, "meet Mr. Knowles, my oldest friend in the world. Vern, this is my son Harvard, and that's my younger boy, Roger." Dad points first to me, still near the window, and then to Roger, who's on the couch. Roger waves at them with both hands.

"Hello there, Roger!" Mr. Knowles waves back, then turns to me. "Harvard, that's a great old Maine name. I hope it suits you as well as it did your great-grandfather. He was a good man. And this is my daughter, Nevaeh. She'll be eleven in October."

"Nevaeh?" I repeat. *Ne-vay-ah*. I never heard that name before.

"Heaven spelled backwards," she explains.

I point a finger at myself.

"Dravrah spelled frontwards."

"Harvard!" Dad scolds.

Nevaeh smiles at me. Her teeth are small and straight and white.

Mr. Knowles belly laughs, and for a split second I'm jealous of Nevaeh, at how easy it is for her father to laugh.

"What are your plans for the summer, Marshall? Lucien hopes you stop by sometime."

"I'll try to. It's up to the boys. On the drive here, Harvard asked what I did in the summers when I lived in Kettle Hole." Dad acts proud at being asked. "I told him how handy my grandfather was and all the projects we worked on in his shop."

"I remember the summer you got interested in bees and found out they were dying off. You and your grandfather made those bee houses, drilling holes in wood, and put them up in the orchard."

"Yes, I remember I drilled my finger pretty good the first try."

"Yes, I recollect that, too! Then there was the summer

your grandfather helped me build the potato rocket cannon. Even he was surprised how far you can launch a potato. Do you have a project in mind, Harvard?" Mr. Knowles asks.

When Mr. Knowles said the word *dying* about the bees, I looked down so I didn't have to see Dad's face. Mr. Knowles sounds like he's hoping I'll ask to build a potato rocket cannon like he did. I'm still looking down trying to come up with an answer when a line of black ants walks past my blue-and-yellow sneakers.

"Ants. I want to do a project about ants," I say.

When I look up, I see Nevaeh is watching the ants, too, and our eyes meet. The ants walk one behind the other, like someone drew a straight line on the floor for them to follow. She doesn't say anything, so I guess this counts as the first secret she keeps for me.

"Me too. I choose ants," Roger says. "Ants and a swimming pool."

Dad claps his hands. "This is exactly the kind of inspiration I was hoping for! I had an ant farm when I was a kid! I think it was a birthday present. Would you boys like to build an ant farm?"

"Why not," I say.

"Why not," Roger says. "What's an ant farm?"

"It's a way to view and study the ant world. First thing tomorrow, I'm going to send away for mail-order ants, and we can get started building our own ant farm. What a wonderful idea, Harvard!"

Dad acts more excited than I've seen him in five months.

After the mistake, Dad did the cooking and cleaning and helped with homework, but he never wanted to play video games or board games or even cards.

Nevaeh gives me another look, her brown bird eyes bright. Neither one of us points out that there are probably enough ants crawling along the floor of the living room to populate a very big ant farm. Even though the ants are walking right past Dad and Mr. Knowles and Roger, somehow Nevaeh and I are the only ones who see them.

"What are *you* interested in, Nevaeh?" Dad asks her.

Nevaeh starts to speak, and coughs, then coughs again and again.

"Nevaeh taught herself to read when she was four," Mr. Knowles tells Dad. "She writes poems, too. Writes me one every year on my birthday. And of course she wrote ones for Earlene, too, before she passed away."

"Do you want a cough drop?" Roger smiles at Nevaeh from the couch, and you can see he's missing his two top front teeth.

"A cough drop?"

"Yeah, for your cough. You're coughing. Just like Mommy does sometimes. Ack, ack, ack, ack." He imitates her. It's true. Mom has asthma, and when she gets a cold, she makes the same barky sounds Nevaeh made.

"No, thank you," she says. "Cough drops don't help this kind of cough."

Through the tall farmhouse windows, I see flashes of light. The sky lights up again and again, as if someone is turning a light switch on and off.

"Heat lightning," Nevaeh says. "It comes from so far away you can't hear the thunder."

"Heat lightning. Is that one word or two?" I ask.

"Two words. If we go outside, we can see it better."

"I'm coming, too." Roger follows us.

Me and Roger and Nevaeh sit on the porch step and watch the sky light up again and again with streaks of silent lightning.

"Very cool," I say. "I never saw this before."

"It'll probably rain soon," Nevaeh says. "I hope it does, because then the air will be less muggy. Muggy air is hard to breathe."

"You sound like a weather forecaster."

"I am, and I control the weather, too, Dravrah," she says in a pretend-serious voice.

I laugh, and Roger asks her, "Can you make it snow?"

"That could be tricky in the summer, but I'll work on it," she answers.

"Yes!" Roger shouts.

The sky lights up again, and it starts raining. Nevaeh and I scramble onto the porch chairs and out of the rain. She takes a pencil and a folded envelope from her back pocket, hunches over, and writes, the pencil gripped in her left hand.

Roger goes out in the yard and throws his arms in the air.

"You did it. You made it rain," he tells her, confusing weather forecaster with weather maker.

"Did you write a poem? Can I see it?" I ask Nevaeh when she stops writing.

At first I think she's going to say no, but then she hands

me the envelope. I read what's written on it, in very small printed handwriting.

> heat lightning is kind
> it doesn't scare you with a boom
> it just blinks its flashlight glow
> across your living room

"That's really good," I say, "and it's exactly right. How the heat lightning is, I mean."

"Thanks." She holds her hand out for the envelope and I give it back.

"Do you miss your home?" she asks.

"A little. My mom is still there. And my best friend Tobias lives down the block, but he's visiting his grandparents in the Philippines this summer."

"How do *you* like it here?" Nevaeh asks Roger.

"The stairs are creaky," Roger says.

"Can you count to twelve?" she asks him.

"One, two, three, four, five, six, seven, eight, nine, ten, eleven, twelve."

"I guess you can. So count the steps when you go up and don't walk on numbers two and nine. Then it won't creak anymore."

"Okay. Two and nine." Roger counts them on his fingers. "Where do you live?" he asks, flashing her his missing-tooth smile.

"I live in the barn," she says, pointing toward the path through the woods.

FOUR

Harvester Ants

The day after I meet Nevaeh, Dad takes me and Roger into town. Town is one long block.

On one side of the block, the signs say AGWAY HARDWARE STORE, BOB'S BARBER SHOP, and KETTLE HOLE BOOKS, NEW & USED. The bookstore sign has a drawing of a black kettle with books in it. And on the other side are a gas station, a bank, a post office, an IGA grocery store, and Cone Heaven.

"Ice cream," Roger announces. He doesn't need to read the words on the Cone Heaven sign because there's a huge cutout of an ice cream cone on the front of the shop, with colored lights for sprinkles on top. There are also people sitting outside at picnic tables eating real life-sized ice cream cones.

I choose a plain vanilla cone, and Roger picks half Maine

blueberry and half mint chocolate chip. Dad doesn't get anything. We're sitting at one of the picnic tables, and Roger starts eating his cone from the bottom and top, as always.

Dad watches Roger's ice cream cone strategy, then stands up.

"I'll get more napkins and ask for a bowl."

When Dad's on line, Roger says, "If Mommy was here, she'd get a hot fudge sundae and let me have a spoonful."

"That's true. She would."

Then he says what I was just thinking.

"And she'd give *you* the cherry."

A man at the next table calls out to us. "Is that Marshall Corson you came with?"

"Yes," I say. "He's our father."

"Thought I recognized him. Left to become some kind of big-city doctor, right?"

"Yes, he's a doctor," I say.

"He back for good? The town could use another doctor up to the clinic."

"Only for the summer," I say.

"Well, that's the way," the man says, nodding. "The little one takes after his father, doesn't he?"

The man points to Roger. It's true that Roger looks more like Dad, who has white, freckled skin and brown hair. I have black hair and brown skin like Mom, and she says I look just like her younger brother Emilio when he was my age.

Roger lifts his ice cream–covered face to the man.

"I'm not little. I'm five."

"Well, sorry about that, little man, I guess you are." The

19

man laughs a kind laugh and waves goodbye to us when he leaves.

We shop for ant farm construction materials at Agway and then stop in Kettle Hole Books. Dad disappears into the upstairs of the bookstore while Roger pets a striped cat who has its own cat bed in the front window display.

Back at the house Dad unpacks the pieces of wood, boxes of nails and screws, and sheets of sandpaper from Agway. Wrapped in brown paper and covered in cardboard are two panes of glass.

Then he lifts a huge book out of the other bag. He holds it up in the air and actually kisses it before he shows it to us.

"Here is the definitive text. I found it on the bottom shelf of the bookstore in the Insects and Amphibians section," he says as he passes it to me.

It's very heavy and says *The Natural Genius of Ants* in black letters on the gold cover.

"Boys," Dad says, "we'd better start building their home, because I chose expedited shipping and the ants are ON THEIR WAY." He says each word of *on their way* slowly, like the ants are almost at our door. The house ants hurry in a straight line up the wall of the living room, right in front of Dad, and disappear into a crack.

"I'm ANT-icipating their arrival," I say.

Dad smiles at my ant joke.

"Maybe Nevaeh will be interested in observing the ants, too."

"Sure," I say. I've been thinking about Nevaeh ever since she visited. How when she leaned forward her hair fell in

20

her face like a curtain closing at the end of a play. How she pressed her hands down on the stone steps to the porch while she looked out at the woods. How she kept the secret of the ants.

"Sure," Roger agrees. "She made it rain and stopped the stairs from creaking. I bet she knows all about ants, too."

In *The Natural Genius of Ants*, there are brown ant-sized stains on the edges of some of the pages, but no ants, alive or dead. I read for a while, turning the sour-smelling pages.

"Dad, what kind of ants are we getting?" I ask. "I hope not fire ants. Because they have poison they inject into other insects and people."

"No, the ants that are coming are western harvester ants. They're not poisonous."

This makes me think. If one of the western harvester ants gets loose and meets our house ants, how would they get along? If they fought each other, how would Dad feel about our summer project turning into an ant battle? Would it get bloody? And do ants even have blood in their bodies?

"What did you feed your ants when you were little?" I ask him.

"Hmm . . . ," he says. "It was a long time ago. I was probably Roger's age when I got the ant farm. I do remember giving them pieces of fruit and bread." Dad comes over and puts his hand on the cover of *The Natural Genius of Ants*. "But I suspect your answer is inside here."

"Thanks, Dad. And do you know if *bloodbath* is one word or two?"

He's rummaging in the desk drawer in the corner of the room and doesn't seem to hear me.

"Here it is! Exactly what we need for this project." He holds up a measuring tape. I knew there was a reason I packed it," he says.

Dad did a good job packing us to go to Kettle Hole. He made a list on his pad and checked off toothbrushes and toothpaste, clothes and pajamas, bathing suits, Roger's life jacket, warm sweaters just in case, sheets, blankets, pillows, and food. He attached our bicycles to a rack on the back of the car. We were about to leave when he held his pen over the last thing on his list. Then he went upstairs to the apartment again, came down with his doctor bag, and put it in the trunk.

There was one thing we couldn't have brought with us, even if Dad had thought of it.

The thing that Roger counted on to help him go to sleep each night. Mom's hand. Since he was little, Mom sat in a rocking chair next to Roger at bedtime and held his hand until he fell asleep.

The first night, on the way to Kettle Hole, Roger slept in the car. The second night, after our first real day in Maine, he fell asleep on the couch.

Tonight, the third night, Roger makes it very clear something essential is missing.

"I need Mommy's hand," he says the second Dad turns off the light in his room.

"I can hold your hand," Dad offers.

"Not *your* hand," Roger answers.

"How about I sit next to you?" I hear the scraping of a chair. "Are you sure you don't want me to hold your hand?"

"No."

Roger sniffles the way he does when he's about to cry.

"I can tell you a story," Dad says.

"About here, when you lived here," Roger demands.

There's more sniffling and then Dad starts speaking.

"When I turned five, like you are, it was January, and my grandfather took me ice fishing for the first time. He said if I caught a fish, we would cook it for supper. I didn't like fish all that well, but I wanted to be the one to catch our supper. I'd never walked on a frozen lake before. As we made our way across, the ice made loud cracking and booming sounds and they scared me. . . ."

Dad stops talking and it's very quiet, except for the chirping sounds of the wood frogs Dad calls *peepers*. I hear him come into the hallway, so I'm guessing Roger fell asleep. I never heard this story before. I want to know how it ends. Why did the ice make those noises? Did he catch a fish? And is *ice fishing* one word or two?

Most of all, though, I'm glad that Dad's story worked the way Mom's hand did.

FIVE

Not-Live Ants

Dad and Roger are in town food shopping when a brown United Parcel Service truck leaves a package on the porch. It's from ANTLIFE INC! and the front of the package says:

URGENT! OPEN IMMEDIATELY!

The live ants got here faster than Dad expected. I'm sure he won't mind me opening it right away. After all, that's what the package says to do. And I figure the ants will want to be let out to see their new home. Or the pieces of wood and glass on the table that will be their new home. When I open the package, a clear plastic tube with a red stopper is attached to a yellow pamphlet that says **LIVE HARVESTER ANTS ENCLOSED** on the front.

Only the live ants don't look alive.

None of the ants in the tube are moving.

The paper that comes with them says:

Your ants might be sluggish.

I gently turn the tube, hoping maybe they fell asleep on the ride here, the way Roger does on long car trips, but they just slide against each other, and none of their many legs move.

These ants are more than sluggish.

The paper also says:

If your ants arrive in cold weather,
you should let them warm up and
they'll become more active.

It's June and pretty hot out already, but I move the tube to the window and hold it up to the sun. Then I blow on it with my warm breath. Still no movement.

I take the ants and the package they came in and go upstairs to my room. I hide them both on a shelf in the closet and cover them with a T-shirt.

Then I lie on my bed and stare at the ceiling, which has thin cracks in the shape of a jellyfish. For once I have nothing to say. Dad is going to build an ant farm for ants that are dead. How can I tell him the ants are dead? When the baby died, I heard Dad say to Mom, "Five months. She only had five months on this earth." Maybe the ants they shipped were already very old, almost-dead ants. I don't know how long ants live, but I can already hear Dad's reply if I ask about that.

"I suspect your answer is inside here."

I go back downstairs and open *The Natural Genius of Ants*, searching through its ant-stained pages. It has a lot of facts about ants:

There are at least 15,000 kinds of ants.

Some are as small as a grain of sand, and some are as big as your thumb.

Some people eat ants.

Finally, I find what I'm looking for:

Queen ants can live from one to twenty years, but adult ants only live a few months.

The paper that came with the ants says:

All the ants we send you are nonbreeding worker ants. The government does not allow shipment of queens.

I don't think they'd ship baby ants, either, so I'm guessing the harvester ants are adults. If ants only live a few months, when do they get to be an adult? At one week old or one month old? And what is a few months? Two or three or five?

When I look up from the book, the black ants are making their way up the wall next to the window again. That's when I get the idea. If I can fill the tube with our house ants, I won't have to tell Dad the western harvester ants died. It might be hard to catch them and get them in the tube, though. I could use an extra set of hands. And I know the perfect person to help me, if she will—Heaven spelled backwards. Roger might be right that she knows all about ants. If she can make it rain, catching ants should be easy as pie.

I run along the path through the woods where Nevaeh pointed and come to a tall barn. On top of the roof there's a square little house, and on top of the little house a weather-vane spins around and around.

Nevaeh is standing under a tree with shaggy, peeling bark. High up on the trunk, branches stick straight out like snowmen arms. She's waving a lit cigarette back and forth in front of her face.

"It's the last one," she says.

"I've heard it's very hard to quit," I sympathize.

She stubs the cigarette out in a metal can on the ground, then carefully slips it into a cigarette pack and puts the pack in her pocket.

"It was the first promise I made to my mom before she died. Not to smoke," she says.

"So what were you doing with the cigarette?"

"Just smelling it," she says, then adds, "Mom smelled like smoke."

"How many promises?" I ask.

"What do you mean?"

"You said *first promise.*"

"Two promises for me. And one for my dad." She doesn't say what the other ones are. Instead, she points to *The Natural Genius of Ants* in my arms.

"Ant book?"

"How did you know?"

"Giant ant on the cover."

I look down at the book and sigh.

"What?" she asks, and sits in a lawn chair under the tree. I only met Nevaeh yesterday, but the way she says the one word, *what*, makes me want to talk. I sit in another chair and tell her about the not-live-ant delivery and the unbuilt ant farm. I say I don't want my father to know about the dead ants, but I don't say why. She's very quiet when she listens, except for when she coughs. When I stop talking, all I hear is the wind blowing through the trees. Even the wind is windier in Kettle Hole. It feels like it's blowing straight into my ears.

"Can I see your book?" she asks. "Maybe there's something in there that can help us."

"Sure. I would have looked it up, but I wanted to get your ideas first. Since it's really your house the ants are living in."

Her hair falls in front of her as she bends over *The Natural Genius of Ants*, turning page after page.

"You're a fast reader. Did you really teach yourself to read at four years old?" I ask.

"Yes. When you ask for the same book every night, it's not hard."

"Let me guess. *Goodnight Moon?*"

"No. *Your Very First Horse*," she says, and smiles. Then she points in the direction of the house. "Which room are you sleeping in?"

"The one with the jellyfish shape on the ceiling."

"You mean the one with the sun's rays shining down on earth," she says, then looks right at me. "Jellyfish is good, too. I didn't think of that."

I wish she'd take a paper and pencil out of her pocket and write another poem. I liked watching her write the heat lightning one. She had the same expression on her face as when she waved the cigarette in the air, like she was seeing something no one else could see.

"Why is there a house on top of the barn?"

"That?" She looks where I'm pointing. "It's a cupola. For ventilation."

"Oh," I say. I was hoping she'd say it was a clubhouse, and we could climb up there.

"These trees are tall." I point to the tree above us and to a woods full of the same shaggy-barked trees between the barn and the road.

"The sugar maples? Yeah, they're really old. Dad calls them the Don't Cut 'Em trees because my grandfather said not to tap them or cut them for firewood, that they might have more value in them than the sugar."

"Tap them?"

"The sap inside the trees is sweet and you can boil it down to make maple syrup or maple sugar."

The sugar maple we're sitting under has a hollow in its trunk near the bottom.

"See that hole? Maybe your grandfather hid gold coins or some other kind of treasure in there," I suggest.

"I've checked," Nevaeh says, "and all I found were porcupine quills. No treasure."

"Maybe your grandfather filled a metal box with money and chained it to a branch high up in a tree. If I were hiding treasure, that's what I'd do. And then I'd leave some kind of mark to remember where it was."

"I think we would have seen that in the winter when the leaves were gone."

She looks at *The Natural Genius of Ants*, touching the big ant on the cover.

"You're really into this ant farm thing."

"My dad is pretty excited about it."

She goes back to reading. Finally, she closes the book, lifts her hair to the top of her head, then lets it fall.

"We can put new ants in the tube. The ants in the house are probably worker ants like the western harvester ants. All the worker ants are female, and they're the ones who scavenge for food. Maybe that's what they are doing in there— looking for food."

"Okay," I say, "let's get some workers."

SIX

Ant Poetry

When we get to the house, Dad is taking a huge flat cardboard package out of the car. Roger follows behind holding a small paper bag.

"Look! It's chalk. And an eraser." Roger pulls a box of colored chalk out of the bag and shows it to us. "And, Nevaeh," he says, "I'm still waiting."

"What are you waiting for?"

"For the snow."

"I'm working on it, Roger. It might take a little more time."

"I know." He nods at her, very seriously. "You have all the other weather to do, too."

In the house, Dad slowly unwraps the package. Instead

of ripping open the cardboard, he takes a small penknife out of his pants pocket, unfolds the blade, and makes careful cuts down each side and across the top. Finally, he lifts out a very large blackboard.

I put both hands over my heart and take a giant step backwards to show how amazed I am.

Dad picks up a piece of yellow chalk and holds it in the air.

"I got this for our ant project! I had a blackboard myself growing up. In my opinion, it's far superior to a whiteboard. Say you're sitting there on the couch, and a question comes to mind. Or a fleeting thought. One that might vanish unless you preserved it. What do you do?"

Dad answers his own question.

"You write it down. And there it will be for everyone else to think about and ponder. It will be a way to share our thoughts. For instance, last night as I was falling asleep, I thought, *How far do ants see?*"

He takes the chalk and writes on the blackboard.

How far do ants see?

While Dad's writing, Nevaeh and I turn our heads to check the edge of the living room floor. Sure enough, a line of black ants moves along the wall. They're walking faster than the last time we saw them. In the ant book it said the biggest colony of ants was a supercolony (or super colony?) with three hundred and six million worker ants, but that was in Japan. I can't imagine how long it took to count all of them, especially if they moved as fast as these ants.

"Dad," I say, lifting up *The Natural Genius of Ants*, "I suspect your answer might be in here."

"Can I write something, too?" Roger says as he reaches for the chalk.

"Of course!" Dad says.

Below Dad's question, Roger writes:

Do Ans Slip?

Dad looks puzzled.

"Would you like to read that to us, Roger?" he asks.

"Do ants sleep?" Roger says, as if it's obvious.

"That's a very thoughtful question. I suppose all living things have to rest to rejuvenate their systems, regardless of how small. But we can research the answer."

"Congratulations, Roger." I pat him on the back. "You just skipped kindergarten! You may be five, but I'm moving you into first grade."

"Yeah!" Roger cheers. "I'm going to call Mommy and tell her RIGHT NOW!" he says, and heads to the desk, where Dad has Mom's cell phone number written in black marker on a big index card taped next to the phone. That's so Roger can talk to Mom whenever he wants, even though she calls me and Roger almost every day before we go to bed. After supper is Dad's time with Mom, when he heads out to the porch or the hammock with his cell phone.

Nevaeh and I go upstairs. Without looking down, Nevaeh skips steps two and nine on the way up. In my room she stretches her neck to look at the ceiling. I do, too. Now that she told me it looked like a sun shining down its rays, that's what I see instead of a jellyfish.

"Sun. Right?" she says.

"Jellyfish *and* sun."

I bring out the test tube with the red stopper.

"Ants. Dead ants, I think. And this came with them." I unfold the yellow pamphlet to where it says:

Welcome to your western harvester ants.

Nevaeh puts her face up to the tube. The reddish-orange ants are stiff and none of their legs or antennae move. She squints, scrunching up her forehead.

"They're definitely dead. Should we bury them?"

I put the tube in my pocket.

"Okay. We can dig a hole and bury them outside. But Roger is going to want to come if he sees us go outside."

"Then let's climb down from the roof," she says.

"How do we do that?"

She opens the window facing the roof, takes out the screen, and climbs out like she's done it a thousand times before.

"This roof to the porch roof and then down the arbor."

I didn't realize the sloping roof outside my window

was only a short jump to the shingled porch roof. I follow Nevaeh down the arbor, which is like a wooden ladder with vines growing on it. When she gets to the ground, she bends over and takes a puff from a red inhaler. Then she stands up and points to a place under the bushes in front of the house.

"How about over there?"

"Sure," I agree.

Nevaeh finds a stick and digs into the dirt to make a small hole. I take the tube out of my pocket, pull off the stopper, and gently pour the ants into the hole. We both use our hands to cover the hole with dirt and pat it down.

"I hope you had a good life," she says to the little mound of dirt that covers the ants. "That's what Dad said to Mom after she died. *I'll love you forever, Earlene. I hope you had a good life.*"

Did Dad say anything to the baby after she died? Something like, *I'm sorry. Even though it was short, even though it was only five months, I hope you had a good life.*

"What do you think a good life is for an ant?" I ask Nevaeh.

"Being with other ants?" she suggests.

"Yeah, and maybe finding food they like to eat or following other ants around."

I put the empty tube back in my pocket.

"I'll let you know when the coast is clear so you can come over and help me get some of the house ants in the tube."

When we go back in the house, the big blackboard is

35

hanging on a wall in the living room. I stop and pick up a piece of chalk. Below **DO ANS SLIP?**, I write:

Which came first, the anteater or the ant?

Nevaeh watches me chalk my question on the blackboard. Her left hand taps against her leg. I pass her a piece of chalk.

"You can write on the blackboard too, if you want."

She draws lines down her right hand, like she's testing it out. Then I hear the squeaks of the chalk while she writes. When she steps back, I read the second poem I've seen from Nevaeh:

does an ant feel big
or does an ant feel small?
or maybe ants don't think about
what size they are
at all.

SEVEN

Camponotus pennsylvanicus

While Dad and Roger are in the tall grass at the edge of the lawn where it meets the woods, Nevaeh and I are trying to get the ants in the tube.

It's hard to get ants in a tube.

My idea: Put the tube in front of where the ants are going, and they'll walk right into it.

Only, they stop, shake their antennae at the entrance to the tube, and change direction.

Nevaeh's idea: Put food in the tube, and the ants will go in to eat it.

We look in *The Natural Genius of Ants* to see what ants eat.

They eat: sugar, seeds, termites, flesh of other dead insects, fruit, oil, grease, and fungus.

"What they eat depends on what kind of ants they are," Nevaeh says, "so first we need to figure out what kind these are."

In the middle of *The Natural Genius of Ants,* there are pages and pages of color photos of ants. We put the book on the floor near the ants and turn the photo pages. There are so many different kinds of ants. Thief ant. Sugar ant. Pharaoh's ant. The house ants have six legs but all ants have six legs, so that doesn't help. We narrow it down to ants that live in Maine, ants that are black, and ants that go in houses.

"Carpenter ants. *Camponotus pennsylvanicus.*" Nevaeh touches a photo. "Look!"

She's right. Our ants look like the black carpenter ants in the book. They have big heads with long antennae, skinny middles, and oval-shaped abdomens with darker black stripes.

"What's the *camponotus* whatever thing you read?" I ask her.

"It's the Latin name for carpenter ants," Nevaeh, lying almost flat on the floor, reads from the book. "Carpenter ants chew through wood to make tunnels, but they don't eat the wood. They eat plant and fruit juices, dead insects, insect parts, honey, eggs, meat, cakes, and grease."

I open the refrigerator.

"We're out of juice and insect parts. Dad uses the eggs for French toast. And Roger ate all the grease. Only kidding, but we do have honey."

Nevaeh sits up, takes a deep breath, and starts coughing. Her face is red.

"Do you want a glass of water?"

"Do you have any coffee?"

"There's some left in the bottom of the coffee machine. I didn't know kids in Maine drank coffee. Do you want honey with it?"

"Do I look like an ant?" Nevaeh laughs, then starts coughing again.

"Honey is good for a cough," I say.

"Is it?"

"Well, did you ever hear an ant cough?"

"Very funny! When my grandmother was wheezy, she'd make herself a cup of coffee. She said it helped her breathing and cost way less than medicine."

I pour the coffee into a blue mug, squirt a few drops of honey in it, and hand it to Nevaeh. She drinks it slowly, then hands the mug back to me.

"Thanks," she says, without coughing.

I look out the kitchen window to make sure Dad and Roger aren't heading back to the house.

"What are they doing?" Nevaeh asks.

"It looks like they're picking flowers now."

Nevaeh holds up the tube.

"Why don't you squeeze a little honey in here?"

I squirt honey into the tube. Some drips onto the floor. And as if the ants have a honey radar alert system, all of a sudden there's a group of ants next to the honey. Before

I can figure out what to do next, Nevaeh gets a piece of construction paper and a paintbrush from the shelf over the desk. She twists the paper into a funnel shape, gently brushes the ants into it with the paintbrush, and fits the small end of the funnel in the top of the tube. When the ants drop into the tube, she plugs it with the stopper.

"Wow! How did you do that so quick? Are you some kind of secret ant wrangler?"

"No. It's the same with horses."

"Horses?" I don't see how there's anything the same between ants and horses.

"When you want to do something with a horse, you have to be the one in charge. My dad says they're herd animals, and someone has to be the boss, so it better be you. Say you need to get a horse in a trailer. You have to lead with confidence, he says, or the horse will sense you're not sure of yourself. I figured if the ants like to follow each other, they might be a herd animal, too."

"Or a herd insect."

Some of the ants in the tube are on the honey and some are climbing the sides. I try to count them and only get up to seventeen because they're moving so much. The tube of ants feels warm in my hand, like they're generating ant heat. Nevaeh watches them, too.

"My old horse, Joker, would follow me everywhere I went," she says.

"Where's Joker now?"

"He's at a camp somewhere. I had to give him back this winter because horse hay doesn't come cheap. He's a camp horse."

"What's a camp horse?"

"It's a horse kids ride at summer camp. At the end of the summer, he was mine for free, until the next summer. Dad called him my winter horse, a horse no one wanted when the weather turned. If we can't pay for his hay, we can't have him back in the fall."

I want to ask more about Joker, but before I can say anything the back door opens. I hide the tube of ants behind my back.

"I picked flowers for Mommy for when she comes." Roger holds out a bouquet. "They're lupines and tiger lilies."

"Very nice," I say.

"What do you think Mommy is doing RIGHT NOW?"

Before I have a chance to say anything, Roger answers his own question.

"I think she's wishing she had flowers from Maine."

Nevaeh looks at the clock on the wall. "I better get home. I'm going shoeing with Dad. Hey, do you want to come with us?" she surprises me by asking.

"Can I?" I ask Dad, even though I have no idea what "shoeing" is. If it's a sport like skiing or snowmobiling that you do in the summer using your shoes. Or if it's the Maine way of talking about shopping for shoes.

"Certainly," he says. "Tell Vern I remember going shoeing with him and his father."

"I've only got my sneakers. Is that okay?" I lift my foot to show Nevaeh.

She gives me a funny look.

"Yes," she says, "if you don't mind them getting dirty."

"Wait for me. I'll be right over," I say, backing my way toward the stairs so no one can see the tube before I hide it in the closet.

EIGHT

Zero Dollars

Nevaeh's dad is in front of the barn house, loading a wooden toolbox into a red truck. The door on the passenger side is gray, and the windshield has wavy cracks in one corner.

"Glad you could join us, Harvard," he says. "How's the ant project going?"

"Good," I say. "We're going to build an ant farm."

"With your dad at the helm, you can count on it being the finest ant farm you ever saw. I once saw a TV show that said there's more ants than humans on earth. So maybe ants have something to teach us," he says.

He puts a short three-legged metal stool with a thick, strange-looking seat next to the toolbox.

"Is that your chair?" I ask Nevaeh.

"It's Dad's stall jack. A portable anvil for hammering horseshoes into the right shape."

Nevaeh climbs in the front seat next to Mr. Knowles and rests her feet on top of the dashboard. I get in next to her, pull the seat belt over my shoulder, and push to hook it, but it won't click in. She sees me trying.

"It's broken."

I think about holding the belt across my lap anyway, but Nevaeh isn't wearing one, either, so I let it go. It's the first time I've ridden without a seat belt.

"What horse are you doing today?" Nevaeh asks Mr. Knowles as we pull out onto the road.

"Going to Lucien Willette's to put new shoes on Frontier Ben," he says.

"Great. I can't wait to see him."

"Why can't he put on his own shoes?" I joke.

Nevaeh and Mr. Knowles laugh.

"He's big, but he's very gentle. I brought him an apple," Nevaeh says, opening the backpack she brought with her. I see the apple and also the pack of cigarettes.

We turn down a dirt road and the glove compartment pops open as we hit the first bump. Nevaeh pushes it shut with her foot, but not before I see a stack of papers stuffed in there.

When we get to the farm, a horse the color of the rust on Mr. Knowles's truck is in the driveway, flicking his tail at a swarm of flies. A man in a green long-sleeved work shirt, orange hat, and dark green pants is brushing flies off the horse's head.

Nevaeh goes right up to the horse, puts both arms around his big head, and touches her nose to his.

"Nevaeh, what happened to my hello?" the man teases her. "It's hard coming second after a horse, even if it is Frontier Ben."

"Hi, Mr. Willette," she says, but doesn't take her eyes off the horse. She runs her hands through Frontier Ben's yellow mane. Mr. Knowles unloads his toolbox from the truck and straps on something that looks like a leather apron.

"You're gonna have to grow some before you can hop on him. You tell your dad to add some grain to your diet. See what it did for Frontier Ben?" Mr. Willette jokes. His beard is almost the color of Frontier Ben's mane, and when he laughs you can see all these deep lines around his eyes.

"What kind of horse is he?" I ask.

"Oh, he's no special breed. Looks like a Belgian, but he's just a Canada bush horse, like my daddy's people used to use on the farms. They're also good at pulling logs."

Mr. Knowles goes over to the big horse, puts his hand on the horse's side, and stands there very still next to him.

"What's he doing?" I whisper to Nevaeh.

"It's to let Frontier Ben know he's there and not to be afraid," she says.

Mr. Willette stands by Frontier Ben's head as Mr. Knowles bends down and picks up the horse's left front foot. He calls out to Nevaeh for tools, one after the other, and she hands them to him from the toolbox.

"Rasp, shoe pullers, hoof pick, hoof knife, nippers, rasp, hoof gauge."

"Doesn't that hurt the horse?" I ask Nevaeh when Mr. Knowles draws the long rasp across Frontier Ben's hoof and then clamps down with the nippers so pieces of hoof fly out.

"No, it's like cutting your fingernails."

Finally, he puts the left front foot down, picks up the right front foot, and asks for the same tools all over again. He does the same thing with Frontier Ben's back feet. Then he puts a horseshoe on the stall jack and bangs on it with a hammer.

After that Mr. Knowles picks up each of the horse's feet and nails a new shoe on each hoof. He keeps the nails sticking out of his mouth and grabs them one at a time when he needs them.

"That doesn't hurt, either?" I ask, wiggling my sneaker in the air.

"Nope. See how calm he is?"

It's true. Frontier Ben stands there patiently while Mr. Knowles lifts each heavy hoof one at a time to work on it. In between hooves, Mr. Knowles wipes the sweat off his face with his sleeve. It looks like hard work bending over with a horse's hoof between your legs or in your lap. Especially one as big as Frontier Ben.

When Mr. Knowles is done, he wipes his face again and sits down on the tailgate of the truck. Mr. Willette leads Frontier Ben through a gate into a field, then comes back, takes a roll of folded-up money from his back pocket, counts out the bills, and gives them to Mr. Knowles.

"Thanks, Lucien," Mr. Knowles says, then points to me. "I should have introduced you before. This is Marshall Corson's oldest boy, Harvard."

"Nice to meet you, Harvard. I heard your father was here. See that barn?" Mr. Willette points to a red barn next to the house. "Your father and Vern and I painted that barn for my father one summer. Vern and I slopped the paint on like there was no tomorrow, and we got one whole side done in a day. Your father, he worked so careful, by nightfall all he'd done was one barn door. Mind you, it was the best job you'd ever seen, but still . . ."

Mr. Willette doesn't finish his sentence. I don't know if he's saying it's a good thing or not, that Dad worked so carefully. It doesn't surprise me that Dad would take all day to paint one door. I guess even then, he wanted his work to be perfect.

Nevaeh slips under the wooden horse fence and goes up to Frontier Ben. With the apple in her palm, her hand flat, she holds it out under the horse's mouth. He bites into it, and when he chews, mushed-up apple pieces fall out. I stay on the not-horse side of the fence.

"You can touch him if you want," she says. So I do. I climb on the lowest rail, lean over, and touch him between his ears. His skin is very soft.

When we get back to the truck, Mr. Knowles and Mr. Willette are looking at something in the grass next to the barn.

"That your snowplow?" Mr. Knowles asks Mr. Willette.

"Yep. It doesn't fit my new truck," Mr. Willette says.

"Are you selling it? I was thinking I could plow driveways this winter, make a little extra cash. Some of my chimney-cleaning customers are looking for a new plow guy."

There is more talk of plows and trucks and snowbanks and snowdrifts and something called *black ice* (or *blackice*), and before you know it, Mr. Knowles is passing back the money he just got from Mr. Willette, and they're loading the plow into the back of the truck.

"I owe you for three more shoeings," Mr. Knowles says.

"Good enough, then." Mr. Willette waves to him as we get back in the truck. Mr. Knowles fishes around in the glove compartment and hands Nevaeh a notebook and a pen. I don't know how he can tell she wants to write a poem.

"Are you going to write a poem about Frontier Ben?" I ask her.

"No, this is Dad's work accounting book," she says, and I read what she writes in her small printed handwriting.

June 20: Shoeing Frontier Ben—0 dollars

We stop at a gas station, and when Mr. Knowles gets out to pump the gas, Nevaeh also gets out on his side, with the notebook and pen.

"I keep track of the gas money, too," she explains.

I put my feet up on the dashboard like Nevaeh did, and the glove compartment pops open again and papers fall out. A few of them are stamped PAID in red ink. And I see the same name on the top of all of them—Earlene Knowles. I shove them back in and close the glove compartment quickly so no one thinks I'm being nosy. That's when I hear Nevaeh say Dad's name.

"Did Mr. Corson really kill someone? That's what

Campbell told me. She said her mother heard it up at the store." Nevaeh's voice carries into my open window from the other side of the truck.

"And how did you answer her?"

"I said you wouldn't have rented out our house to a killer. But she said her mother was positive."

"God bless Campbell's mother," I hear Mr. Knowles say.

"So, did he?"

There's a pause, and when I sneak a look at them from the back window, I see Nevaeh's dad put his hand on top of her head, the same way he touched Frontier Ben.

"Marshall Corson is not a danger to anyone but himself," he says.

NINE

Friend or Enemy?

"Guess what came." I show Dad and Roger the tube full of live house ants. "It said open immediately, so I did. I opened it at the mailbox."

It's a lie, but the truth is worse. I threw out the pamphlet that came with the dead harvester ants, because the picture on the front showed small reddish ants, not big black carpenter ants.

The second Dad sees the ants, he cups his hands together. I put the tube in them.

"Look how big and strong you are," Dad gushes, "and so active! Don't worry, we're going to get your house built in a jiffy. We didn't know you'd get here so quickly."

I imagine Dad talked to his hospital babies in their plastic boxes the same way. Mom said the mothers and fathers of the babies he took care of loved Dad because he treated each baby like it was his own child.

He'd tell us stories when he got home from work. A baby getting held by their mom for the very first time. A baby going home after six months in the hospital. Tiny twin babies learning to drink from a bottle. They were mostly happy endings until the mistake happened.

"You're bigger and not red like the ants I had as a boy." Dad's doctor eyes study them. "But that was a long time ago."

"Let me. Let me hold them and talk to them, too," Roger says.

Dad carefully passes the tube to him.

"Hi, ants, I'm Roger," Roger says, introducing himself. I wait for him to say more, but he just stands there transfixed by the ants. Finally he speaks again.

"How do they do that? How do they walk with all those legs?"

"They're ants, Roger," I explain. "It's easy for them."

Roger gives the tube back to me, then drops to the floor. He tries to move like an ant on all fours, with his bottom and head in the air. Roger's problem is that even with two legs and two arm-legs, it still only adds up to four legs. The ants move like this: front and back legs on one side and the middle leg of the other side in one step. Roger doesn't have a middle leg, so when he tries to move like an ant, he falls on his head. Again and again and again.

"Enough, Roger," Dad warns. "You can't keep falling on your head."

Roger goes outside and comes back wearing his bicycle helmet, which is shiny and black like an ant's head. He goes back to his ant-walking, crashing his helmet head on the floor until he figures out an ant walk that almost matches the real ants.

"Wow, Roger! You're walking like an ant," I say. "I bet we can make antennae for your head, too."

I wiggle my two pointer fingers on top of my head to show him what I mean. *Antennae* is not exactly a first-grade vocabulary word.

"Yes, I need them," Roger agrees.

Dad looks up from the table. He already has the measuring tape in his hand and a pencil behind his ear. The boards and glass pieces are laid out in front of him.

"Why are you wearing your bike helmet in the house, Roger?"

"It's not a helmet. It's my head. My ant head."

Roger ant-walks under the table and across Dad's feet, the way the house ants climb over each other.

"Dad, can you help Roger?" I ask.

"Sure, what do you need help with, Roger?"

Roger taps the top of his helmet, and I explain for him.

"He needs antennae."

Dad goes out to the shed and comes back with a tube of glue, a roll of wire, and wire cutters. He glues two wires to Roger's bike helmet, and they move when he does, just like ant antennae. When I accidentally drop a piece of cracker, Roger ant-walks under my legs and eats it off the floor with his mouth. When he does that, the line of house ants along the wall stop and turn their heads to look at him. Roger keeps going right past them.

It's the most fun we've had so far in Kettle Hole. The kitchen table is covered with ant farm pieces, so instead of a regular supper, Dad serves cut-up apples, mini-pretzels, sunflower seeds, crackers, and hard-boiled eggs on the coffee table in the living room. I eat apple slices on crackers. Except for the fact that there's no insect parts or grease, it's the kind of meal I think a carpenter ant would like.

Roger ant-climbs around the couch. It gets later and later, and the dark—the dark that's darker in Kettle Hole than anywhere else I've been—fills the windows. Dad and I work together.

"Do you think that edge needs more planing?" he asks.

"What about adding another air hole on the side?" I suggest.

When I take a snack break, I look in *The Natural Genius of Ants* to find out more about carpenter ants. *Camponotus pennsylvanicus.*

This is what I find out:

1. They have no eyes or legs when they are born.

2. They are more active at night.

3. They use their antennae to figure out if someone is a friend or an enemy.

The house ants are doing the second and third things. A few of them break out of their line and run up a table leg to watch the ant farm being built. Dad has no idea they're observing his careful measuring and sanding. Another group of ants makes its way past me, close enough so I can see their antennae move back and forth, as if they're trying to figure out if I'm a friend or an enemy.

"Friend," I say quietly. I wish I had antennae to signal back to them, so I do the next best thing—hold up a high five (one word or two?) hand. Now I wish I knew the answer to Dad's blackboard question—**How far do ants see?**—because the ants disappear under the couch without any sign that they understood my message.

Dad forgets brushing-teeth time, pajama time, and bedtime. Roger falls asleep on the rug and I take his helmet off.

When we're done, probably the most perfect ant farm ever is on the kitchen table. It only took one doctor and one and a half assistants five hours to make. It's twelve inches tall by sixteen inches wide by one and a half inches deep, about the size of the *Natural Genius of Ants* book. The pine wood is sanded, and the glass panes are wiped free of smudges. There are round holes with screening to let air in. And a removable top.

"It looks amazing, Dad! If there was a contest for best ant farm, we'd definitely win." I go a little overboard with the praise.

Dad looks pretty happy. "That we might," he says.

"Is it ready for the ants to go in?" I ask.

"We'll need to put the sand in first. Why don't we get that in the morning?" Dad suggests. He bends down and scoops Roger off the floor. Roger keeps sleeping.

"But is it okay to keep the ants in the tube overnight? I don't want them to suffocate and die in there without enough air."

Dad's face changes when I say *suffocate* and *die*. He puts Roger back down on the rug.

"I'll make a breathable cover for the tube."

He cuts a piece of screening, pops off the red stopper, covers the opening with the screening, and tapes it around and around the tube. He's so fast none of the ants at the top of the tube have a chance to get out.

"There we go. All set," Dad says.

"Can I bring the ants upstairs?"

"Sure."

I still don't know how far ants can see, but I hold up the tube so they can watch Dad clear the tools and extra wood off the kitchen table, fill the coffee machine for the morning, and carry Roger upstairs to bed.

When Dad is gone I call Mom's cell from the phone on the desk. Mom must sleep with her phone next to her pillow because she answers on the first ring.

"Harvard! You're still awake? Is everything okay?"

"Yes. We were working on a project. Dad just took Roger up to bed. We have ants."

"Did you say you have ants?"

"Yes."

"Well, you're living in the country now. So ants are probably to be expected. If it becomes a problem, Dad can pick up some ant bait traps in town."

"NO! I mean, it's not a problem. They're going in our ant

55

farm. We built it ourselves. Dad had one when he was grow-ing up, too."

"Oh."

"How's it going with the parasites?"

"Very well," Mom says. "It's wriggling along."

"Okay, just don't let them get too *attached* to you."

"Perfect one, Harvard! I miss you very much. How are things going there?"

"They're good. Roger picked flowers for you," I tell her.

"That's so thoughtful."

"How's Abuela?"

"She's doing fine. She sends her love."

"When are you coming to Maine?"

"I'm hoping to figure out my schedule very soon," Mom answers.

"When is *very soon*?" I ask. "Because the flowers are start-ing to wilt already."

TEN

Ant Naps

With the tube in one hand and the ant book under my arm, I head upstairs. I set them on the nightstand next to my bed and watch the ants in the tube. All except one have their mandibles—*The Natural Genius of Ants* word for *mouth*—in the honey. I can't tell if they're licking it, sucking it up like a straw, biting into it, or stuck to it.

The ant that's not on the honey is halfway up the tube. She's twice the size of the other ants, and she only has one antenna on the left side. The right antenna is missing. I watch her wave her left antenna, and that's when I come up with a name for her—Tenna, short for Antenna. I wave my left hand back at her.

I wish I could communicate with Tenna. I'd ask, Why aren't you eating the honey, too? Are you full, or are you holding out for insect parts or grease? Why are you so much bigger than the other ants? Were you born with only one antenna, or did another ant or insect bite it off?

Unfortunately, I don't think there's a way to give an ant a new antenna, the way Dad attached Roger's antennae to his bike helmet.

My bedroom door opens, and Roger is there.

"Are the ants sleeping?" he asks.

"No, but you should be."

"*You're* not sleeping. Can I stay in here with you and the ants tonight?"

"Okay, get in bed, and I'll look up the answer to your ant question."

Roger gets under my blankets.

"Do you wish we were back home?" Roger pronounces it like it's one word—*backhome*.

"No. Do you?"

"No," he says, and I can tell it's because he wants to say the same thing I did. "I'm leaving half the pillow for you." He pats one side of it.

I lie on the floor on my stomach with the book in front of me the way Nevaeh did.

"Do you miss Mommy?" Roger says.

"You can call her tomorrow," I say. "Would that be good?"

"Yes, because I know she misses me. What do you think she's doing RIGHT NOW?"

I was actually wondering the same thing.

"I think she's sleeping."

"Oh," Roger says. "If Mommy was here and she was awake, she'd say, *What was your favorite part of today, Roger?* And I'd say, *Being an ant.*"

If Mom *was* here in Kettle Hole, I wouldn't have had to explain what I meant by *We have ants*, like I did on the phone.

"I found your answer," I say, after a while.

"What?" Roger answers, rubbing his eyes and yawning.

"Ants don't sleep like we do, but they do nap. They take two hundred and fifty naps a day."

"That's a lot." Roger curls onto his side, taking over the rest of the pillow.

"Yes, but each nap is really short. Only one minute long."

"How long is a minute?" he asks.

"Sixty seconds. I'll count it out, so you see how long it is. One, two, three, four, five, six . . ."

I only get to six before Roger is asleep.

I put on my pajamas and get in bed next to him. Not only does Roger have my whole pillow, but he has most of my blankets, too. I lie there with my head flat on the sheet. The quiet in Kettle Hole is quieter than anything I didn't hear at home. I never knew before how quiet has a sound because the quiet in the room buzzes in my head. I hope Nevaeh is home tomorrow so she can be there to help put the ants in the ant farm. And before I fall asleep, I think of my own ant question to write on the blackboard in the morning.

How can you tell when an ant is napping?

When I wake up, my head is still flat on the sheet. It's raining out, and Roger and the ant tube and *The Natural Genius of Ants* are gone from my room.

Downstairs, Roger is at the table with his eyes closed. A white kitchen timer with its black numbers is ticking in front of him. Dad is writing on the blackboard.

"What's going on, Roger?"

He doesn't answer until the timer goes off. Then he opens his eyes and explains.

"I remembered what you told me about the ants. I was taking a nap. A one-minute nap."

The ants are in their tube next to the ant farm. I bend over and look for Tenna. At first I can't find her. Then I see her in the middle of all the other ants. Her antenna isn't moving, and I don't know if that means she's taking a nap.

Dad steps back from the blackboard, and under the words:

How far do ants see?

he has written in yellow chalk, with his neat writing:

Ants see from one to two feet ahead of themselves.

"Then the ants can see us," I say, more to myself. This means Tenna might have seen me wave my hand.

"Yes. Not much different than newborns, who see eight to fifteen inches in front of themselves," Dad says.

It seems like there's a very big difference between ants and newborns, but maybe not to Dad. This is the first time he's talked about his hospital work since we moved to Kettle Hole. Maybe he's beginning to think of the ants as his new babies.

Which means I'm going to have to keep these ants alive.

I take a piece of chalk and under **DO ANS SLIP?**, I write:

Ants take 250 naps a day. Each nap is about one minute long. Only 20 percent of the ants nap at the same time, so there's always someone awake to guard the colony.

Roger puts on his antennae bike helmet, sets the timer again, lays his head on the table, and scrunches his eyes shut.

Dad studies the blackboard.

"Excellent research, Harvard. Our ant knowledge is expanding exponentially. Are you ready to take a drive to the sandpit?"

"What's a sandpit? Is it anything like an armpit? And is *sandpit* one word or two?"

I half expect Roger to fall out of his chair at the word *armpit*, but he's deep into his ant nap.

"One word. It's where the town digs the sand to spread on the roads in the winter. We can get sand for the ant farm."

The harvester ants that died grew up in the desert and lived in sand, but carpenter ants like rotting logs and stumps and tree bark and wet dirt.

I think fast.

"If the ants are going to live in Maine, why can't we give them a real Maine habitat? With dirt from outside?"

"I don't see why not. They could easily tunnel through dirt, too."

Roger's timer goes off and I head to the door before Dad has a chance to change his mind.

"I'm gonna go see if Nevaeh wants to help collect the dirt," I yell back, and run into the pelting-down rain. In Kettle Hole the rain lands right on the ground, instead of bouncing off stores and sidewalks and tall buildings and highways. There are already puddles in the worn path to Nevaeh's barn. And the rain keeps falling hard, making the perfect habitat for ducks and birds and carpenter ants.

ELEVEN

Mind-Reading Game

I hear voices from inside Nevaeh's barn and knock on the side door.

She lets me in. There's another girl there bouncing a tennis ball off a wooden wall. She's wearing black running shorts and a tank top with brown and black stripes that remind me of the lines the *camponotus pennsylvanicus* have on their abdomens. Her hair is short and black, and her round eyeglasses are purple.

"This is my best friend, Campbell. Her mother and my mother were friends when they were growing up, too. And this is Harvard, who lives next door now." Nevaeh introduces us from the couch, where she's sitting and drinking what looks like coffee.

"You're practicing in case you get a dog?" I ask Campbell, pointing to the ball.

"No, I'm working on my hand-eye coordination. How do you like it in Kettle Hole? You're here with your father, right?"

She says *father* very slowly.

"Yes, me and my father and my brother, Roger. Roger's home right now taking a few naps."

"Oh. My mother said your father was the valedictorian of his class. And that he was the first kid to ever go to the State Spelling Championships and—"

"Campbell, c'mon. Let's play that mind-reading game I was telling you about," Nevaeh says. I get the feeling she's trying to stop Campbell from saying anything else about Dad.

"Harvard, look around if you want," Nevaeh tells me. "Dad fixed up the barn so he could rent out the house. He still has some more work to do."

The barn house is all one room. Big wooden beams cross the ceiling. The walls are wood painted white, and the windows are different sizes. There's a stove in the corner with a pipe going through the wall. A ladder leads to a platform with a railing, and there's a bed up there.

On top of a bookshelf next to a horse bookend are two inhalers like Mom's, an orange one attached to a clear plastic piece that looks like a mini-submarine and a red one.

"I'm thinking of a number between one and ten. Can you guess it?" I hear Nevaeh ask Campbell.

"Aren't we a little old for guessing games?"

"Try it anyway. Just for fun."

"Okay. Seven."

"Wrong," Nevaeh says. "Try again."

"Five," Campbell guesses.

"Wrong again."

"Why do you keep saying *wrong*? It's not like there's a right answer, anyway."

"There *is* a right answer," Nevaeh says. "It's the one I'm thinking of. Guess one more time."

I realize Nevaeh is giving her a big clue when she says it's the *one* I'm thinking of and to guess *one* more time.

"Three," Campbell says.

"Sorry, wrong again."

"I give up. This game is boring."

"The number I was thinking of was one," Nevaeh says.

"Was there a prize if I guessed right?" Campbell asks.

"No, no prize," Nevaeh admits.

"Who sleeps up there?" I ask Nevaeh, pointing up to the loft.

"I do. Dad built the ladder."

"Where does he sleep?"

"On the couch."

"The couch is one of Roger's favorite places to fall asleep. Besides the floor!" I say, and then I remember why I came over.

"Dad finished the ant farm last night. He wanted to put sand in it, but I thought we should collect dirt from around here. You should come see it, too, Campbell."

A car honks, and Campbell catches the ball in one hand.

"My mom's here for me, but I might be able to stop over another time. Are your ants going to hibernate in the winter? I've never seen ants on snow."

"I'll have to look that up," I say. I'm impressed by her question, which definitely belongs on the blackboard.

"Bye, Nevaeh. Bye, Harvard," she says, and the side door bangs shut behind her.

"Campbell didn't get the hints about your number," I say when she's gone.

"No, she didn't. I was working on the second promise."

"What's the second promise?"

"Find a friend who can read your mind. Mom said I should find a friend who can read my mind. I don't know what she meant by that. I wanted to see if it worked with Campbell."

"What about your dad's promise?"

Nevaeh straightens the books between the bookends. The one at the end has a horse on the cover.

"Dad's promise was to pay off the rest of Mom's hospital bills. We lost our health insurance when she had to stop working, and she wouldn't take state aid. She said we weren't beggars and we don't take handouts. They used up their savings and sold Dad's father's antique Farmall H tractor that was in perfect condition."

Now I know why only some of the papers in the glove compartment are marked PAID.

Then I speak before I have a chance to think. "Did your Mom die from a mistake?"

Nevaeh doesn't seem upset at my question. "No, just from being sick."

66

"My mom has an inhaler like that, except for the submarine part."

Nevaeh picks up the orange inhaler and separates it from the long plastic piece.

"It's a spacer, not a submarine. It's for my asthma."

She turns the orange inhaler so I can see a white square at the bottom.

"See, it comes with numbers on it. This one started with one hundred and twenty-four. Each time you take a puff, the number gets smaller."

"It says zero, zero, zero."

"I know. But there might be a little medicine left in the very bottom. See?" She shakes it and squeezes the inhaler. It makes a sound like someone blowing air out of their mouth. I've never used an inhaler, but there's not just one zero on it. There are three of them.

"What about the red one? Does that have numbers, too?"

"Yeah. I only use that one if I'm going on a hike or I pet a dog and it makes me stuffy." Nevaeh hands it to me. "The orange one is for every day."

The red one has a little square, too, but there's only room for one zero. I put it back on the bookshelf.

"Does your dad know your inhalers say zero?"

"No, Mom was the one who used to take me to the clinic. She said we were lucky to have health insurance because just the one orange inhaler cost more than a hundred bales of hay. That's as much as Joker ate in a winter."

"That sounds boring. Eating hay every day."

"Believe me, it's not boring for a horse. Anyway, the

doctor at the clinic said some kids outgrow their asthma. So maybe that will happen to me. I'll wake up one day and it'll be gone. And I won't need any more inhalers."

"Poof." I wave my hand in the air, like I'm making her asthma disappear. "So, do you want to get the dirt now? And after we collect it, I want you to meet someone. Here's a hint. Her name is Tenna."

TWELVE

Hemlock Grove

've never collected dirt in the rain. I've never collected dirt at all. But Nevaeh acts like it's no big deal.

"I'll get us trowels for digging,"

We go in the barn side of the barn house, and Nevaeh swings open a half door you can see over. There's a space half the size of my Kettle Hole bedroom.

"This was Joker's stall," she says.

The stall looks empty the way Mom's side of the bed looks in Dad's room. Like something that should be there is missing.

"Could you get a cat for a pet? They don't eat that much."

Nevaeh shakes her head. "I'm allergic to cats."

"What about dogs?"

She looks even sadder about this question. "Also allergic. I once had a goldfish."

She closes the stall door and looks on a shelf in the barn.

"Here they are." She takes down two tools that look like miniature shovels and puts them in a metal pail. "This should do it for collecting the dirt. And I know a place where the rain won't bother us when we dig," she says.

"A place where you control the rain?" I ask, sounding like Roger.

"No, you'll see," she says, and I follow as she heads toward the trees at the edge of the back lawn, turning onto one trail after the other, taking us deeper and deeper into the woods. The steep paths all lead downhill.

Finally, she stops in a place where the rain doesn't fall on us, and the ground underneath is dry.

"Hemlock grove," she says.

All around us are trees with long drooping branches filled with needles. The branches are so thick they block the rain. The ground is full of light brown cones the size and shape of jellybeans.

"The *camponotus pennsylvanicus* might like a cone to climb on," I say, using my two new Latin words.

"Sure, and the *camponotus pennsylvanicus* might like part of this stump." Nevaeh digs into a moss-covered stump with one of the trowels. The stump crumbles into chunks of rotted wood.

"How about a piece of this bark?" One hemlock tree has

70

holes in its trunk and bark peeling off. "*Camponotus pennsyl-vanicus* love to tunnel in rotting bark."

"Okay, and here's a rock for them to hide behind." Nevaeh holds up a gray pebble.

We drop bark, moss, hemlock cones, pieces of rotten stump, Nevaeh's pebble, and dirt into the bucket. When it's full, each of us holds a side of the wire handle with one hand, and the bucket swings between us as we head back.

"What's Tenna like?" Nevaeh asks. She purses her lips and blows out her breath as we walk back uphill.

"You'll see when you meet her. But I'll say one thing. She's a hard worker."

I can see the Nevaeh mind-wheels turning.

"There's a girl named Annette at school. Is Tenna's name Annet spelled backwards?"

"No, but Annette would be a good name for her, too."

"Or ANTonia?"

When we come out of the woods near the house, the grass is wet, but the rain has stopped.

"By any chance"—the corners of Nevaeh's mouth turn up—"does Tenna happen to like honey?"

When we bring the bucket in, Dad is at the blackboard again, and Roger is watching the ants in the tube. We put the bucket down and some of the house ants crawl up and into it. They quickly disappear under the pieces of bark and moss.

Dad steps away from the blackboard, and I see what he wrote.

How many stomachs do ants have?

_____ 1
_____ 2
_____ 3
_____ 4

"Wow! It's multiple choice! Did you see this, Roger?" I say, then read what's on the blackboard out loud to him.

Roger puts on his ant helmet and falls to the floor in front of Nevaeh. He bends his head so his antennae tap her leg.

"Can you tell what I am?" he asks.

"I'm pretty sure you're an ant."

"Yes!" Roger says, and performs an extra fast ant-run across the room.

"You're a very speedy ant!" she says.

"Look what we found for the ant farm. From a hemlock grove. They're really cool trees," I tell Dad.

He bends down to examine what's in the bucket.

"This looks like great material for the farm. My grandfather said if you got lost in the woods, look at the tops of the hemlocks. They point east because the wind blows from the west."

"I wonder if it's the same for sugar maples. Did you know Nevaeh's grandfather told Mr. Knowles never to cut the maples near the barn? That they might have treasure in them?"

"Oh yes. The Don't Cut 'Em trees." Dad nods like he's remembering hearing the story.

"Did you and Mr. Knowles ever look for the treasure? Maybe his father cut a secret opening somewhere on a trunk of a tree, hid the treasure in it, and covered it with wood to look like bark."

"We didn't think of that," Dad says.

"Here's the ants." I show Nevaeh the tube as if she's never seen it before. I touch the side of the tube near the stopper.

"Nevaeh, this is Tenna." I introduce them the way Nevaeh introduced me and Campbell.

"Hmm. She's really big. And she only has one antenna."

Tenna raises herself up on her back legs and slowly swivels her antenna around, as if she understood what Nevaeh said and wants to show off her bigness and her one antenna.

There's not a lot of room between the two glass sides of the ant farm, so it turns out we have enough dirt and moss and sticks to fill at least ten ant farms. We put the farm on the floor and take turns spooning in the dirt. Nevaeh adds her pebble and Roger drops in a chunk of soft moss. I choose a thick piece of bark and carefully place it on top of the dirt.

"Let's let Nevaeh put the ants in the farm," I suggest. Nevaeh has quick hands like Dad, and she got the ants in the tube, so I think she'd be the best person for the job. I don't mention that the ants already know she's in charge.

"Okay, only because she did the rain," Roger agrees.

Nevaeh must have thought ahead to how the ants would go into the farm, because she makes another construction paper funnel, holds it over the farm, and twists off the red stopper on the tube. The ants slide down the funnel into the ant farm. Tenna is the first one in.

Like she knew I put it there for her, Tenna heads straight under the bark.

Dad and Roger and I watch the ants while Nevaeh reads *The Natural Genius of Ants*. She keeps turning the pages, back and forth, back and forth, like she's hunting for something in particular.

"How inquisitive! How agile!" Dad admires the ants, who are in constant motion. "Look at that one," he points to Tenna. "She's extraordinarily large!"

I think fast.

"I call her Tenna. You know, short for Antenna. Maybe we got her as a special bonus ant because you paid for the expedited shipping?"

"That could be," Dad agrees.

The ants remind me of me and Roger on our first day in Kettle Hole. We went outside to explore the yard, then inside again to see rest of the house, then back outside.

After a while, Dad says, "Let's give them some darkness to adjust to their new home," and he covers the ant farm with a dish towel.

When I look away from the ants, Nevaeh is at the blackboard. There's a check mark next to _2, and underneath Dad's multiple-choice question is written:

Ants have two stomachs. One is their own private stomach and the other one is their social stomach. They use their social stomach to share food with other ants. It might look like kissing, but they are passing food from mandible to mandible.

"Oh no," I groan. "Please don't tell Roger."

"Please don't tell Roger what?" Roger comes over, and then Dad is there, too, reading Nevaeh's answer.

"Please no," I beg.

"Why? You promoted me. I'm in first grade now," Roger says. "You can tell me. What does it say?"

"Nevaeh is absolutely correct." Dad sounds thrilled with Nevaeh's blackboard answer. "Ants do have two stomachs. One for their own food and one they use to share food with other ants. They pass the food from their social stomach with their mandible"—Dad touches his mouth—"to another ant's mandible." Dad gestures with the same hand to an imaginary mandible in the air.

Unfortunately, Roger gets it.

"From their mouth right into another ant's mouth," he says in an awed voice.

There's a rap at the door, and it's Mr. Knowles.

"I figured you'd be over here," he says to Nevaeh.

"Vern, the ants are getting acclimated to their new environment, but you can take a peek at the ant farm. Your daughter was instrumental in the setup."

Dad lifts the dish towel for Mr. Knowles.

"You had to send away for those? What the heck did they charge you? I guess I'm in the wrong line of work." Mr. Knowles laughs and Dad looks confused.

Nevaeh is there next to him in a flash.

"Dad," she says, pulling on her father's arm, "you promised you'd wire a light in the loft so I can read at night. Can you do it now?"

"Okay," he says, letting her pull him over to the door. On the way out, she waves her left hand at me, the way both a left-handed girl and a left-antennaed ant would do.

THIRTEEN

Tunnels

Mom calls after supper and Roger runs over to pick up the home phone. Tonight's call goes the way most of his calls with Mom go. I can only hear his side of the conversation.

Part One:

"Hi, it's Roger."

"I'm good. I want to leave you a message."

"But I don't want to hang up."

"It's a surprise message. I can't tell it now."

"Then you hang up first."

"Okay. Call me when you get my message."

Part Two:

"Hi, Mommy, it's Roger. I'm leaving a message for you. The message is to call me."

Roger asks for the fishing story every night now, and it works to put him right to sleep. Dad tells it almost exactly the same way, and stops the story when Roger falls asleep. Tonight Dad gets this far.

"When I turned five, like you are, it was January, and my grandfather took me ice fishing with him for the first time. He said if I caught a fish, we would cook it for supper. I didn't care for fish all that well, but I wanted to be the one to catch our supper. As we made our way across the lake, the ice made loud cracking and booming sounds and they scared me. My grandfather pulled the hand auger, the tip-ups, the sieve, and the bait on a sled."

Dad's story doesn't work for me. I can't fall asleep. Hours pass and it's still Kettle Hole dark. At home, if I couldn't sleep, I'd get up and walk around the apartment. No matter how quiet I was, Mom would usually hear me. We'd have a snack from her secret stash, and she'd ask what I was thinking about that kept me from sleeping.

Tonight I'm thinking about the *Camponotus pennsylvanicus* in the ant farm. I keep wondering what they're doing under the dish towel downstairs and if Tenna is chewing on the bark.

I also think about the promises Nevaeh made to her mother—not to smoke and to find a friend who could read her mind. Then there's the promise Mr. Knowles made—to pay what it cost when Earlene was sick.

If I could make people keep promises for me, what would I choose? I would make Roger promise not to fall on his head anymore. For Dad's promise, I would ask him to forgive himself for his mistake. For Mom's promise, not to forget there are four people in our family.

I think my way downstairs, minus steps two and nine. Instead of turning on the bright overhead light, I switch on the standing lamp in the corner next to the desk. Then I head straight to the ant farm and lift up the dish towel. I spot Tenna right away. She's still under the bark. And I see the most amazing thing—where yesterday there was packed-down dirt, now there's a brand-new curving tunnel about the size of my little finger. All the ants except Tenna are hard at work in the tunnel, picking up and carrying out clumps of dirt in their mandibles. Some of the pieces are as big as their heads.

How long will the tunnel be? Who decides when it's done? Do they take a vote? Do the ants who carry smaller pieces of dirt get in trouble from the ants carrying bigger loads? Why is Tenna lying there watching everyone else work? Is she napping? Dad might have to get me my own blackboard for all my questions.

The measuring tape Dad used to build the ant farm is in the top drawer of the desk. I stretch it out the length of the tunnel, then write on the blackboard.

Tunnel Progress—3:30 a.m.—2^1/$_2$ inches

When I put the measuring tape back, I notice a stack of papers in the drawer with Dad's handwriting on them.

One says:

Dear McKenzie,
I'm so sorry.

Another one says:

Dear McKenzie,
I wish I had words

And the last one:

Dear McKenzie,
When I think of

I pick up the home phone and call Mom.

"Harvard, it's three-thirty a.m. Is something wrong?"

"You said I could call anytime. Now is when I wanted to call."

"I see. How are you doing?"

"The ants made a tunnel that's two and a half inches long."

"That's very industrious of them." Mom pauses for a second. "Is that why you called?"

"Who's McKenzie?" I ask.

There's a longer pause and I hear Mom breathing.

"The baby's mother. Did someone say something to Dad?"

She doesn't have to say which baby's mother. We both know which one.

"No one said anything. I found letters Dad started writing. I think he wants to say sorry to her."

"It's not that simple."

That's another thing people say about mistakes that's not true.

Just say sorry.

"Why not?"

"His lawyer doesn't want him to do that. It's complicated," she says.

"You said the same thing twice. *It's not simple* is the same thing as saying *it's complicated.* So if I understood *it's not simple*, you didn't need to say *it's complicated.*"

"Can we discuss this in the daylight, Harvard?"

"What's going to be different in the daylight?"

"I'm half-awake now. Hopefully I won't be so tired then."

"Hopefully you won't be so tired, and you'll be more than half-awake. That's saying the same thing twice, too."

Mom sighs almost loud enough for me to hear six states away, and I feel bad that I woke her up.

"Don't tell Dad what I said about the letters," I say.

"I won't. But this is not something for you to worry about."

"I'm not worried."

"That's good, because you don't need to be," she says. "How's your brother? He left me a message saying he was going to leave me a message, but he never did. Something about his bike helmet?"

"He's been wearing his bike helmet," I say.

"That's good to hear. Safety first."

"Kind of."

"I'll call him tomorrow. I know it's hard for us to be

separated like this. Let's talk again soon. I love you with all my heart."

"I love you, too," I answer before I hang up. Now that I know who McKenzie is, my Harvard mind-wheels are turning. It's like I've been given a clue, but I have no idea what to do with it.

FOURTEEN

Hail in July

"You must have been up during the night, and the ants were, too," Dad says when I come downstairs the next morning. He points to the tunnel measurement on the blackboard, and then to the tunnel in the ant farm. It now ends in a hollowed-out chamber that's wider than the tunnel itself. The carpenter ants carry bits of dirt out of the tunnel in their mandibles. Tenna is still under the bark.

When Dad sets a cup of milk in front of Roger, he lifts his arms up and puckers his lips. His cheeks are puffy, and I have a strong suspicion I know what's going to happen next. Dad leans down to kiss him, and when their lips get close, a little pretzel passes out of his mouth toward Dad. Dad pulls back.

"Take it, Dad." Roger's words come out muffled, because he's still holding the pretzel between his teeth. "It's from my social stomach."

Dad hesitates, and I suspect his doctor brain is thinking about what kind of germs a saliva-soaked pretzel might have versus encouraging Roger's interest in ants. The germs win. Dad takes the pretzel from Roger's mouth with two fingers.

"Can I save it for later?" he asks. "For a snack?"

Roger thinks that over.

"Okay, you can eat it and keep it in your private stomach. You don't have to give it to anyone else."

Then Roger leans toward me and another pretzel pokes out of his mouth. The house ants stop and turn toward us, and maybe that's what makes me do it. It's like they're challenging me. I take the edge of the soggy pretzel between my teeth and swallow it very quickly.

"Yum," I say.

The house ant at the front of the line gets up on its back legs and claws its other four legs in the air, which I think might be ant for clapping or cheering.

Roger beams at me, then another pretzel slips out between his lips.

"Thanks, Roger, I'm full," I say, rubbing my private stomach to make the point extremely clear.

I take my first bite of French toast when I notice Roger leaning over the ant farm. Dad is smiling at the ants as he watches them move in and out of the tunnel. Roger's hand inches toward the ant farm cover.

"Roger!" I warn him, quoting from the live-ant pamphlet, "It's not good to overfeed ants. They only need to be fed once every few days."

I point to the glob of honey stuck to the side of the glass wall and the sliver of apple already turning brown on top of the dirt. "See, they have plenty to eat for now."

But Roger isn't looking at the ant farm anymore. He's staring out the window. I look up and see snowballs the size of marbles falling. Then there's a loud *tap-tap-tap* sound of them hitting the house.

"Look, she did it! Nevaeh made it snow for me," he cheers.

He runs to the front door, and when he opens it, Nevaeh is there, bent over, with her hands on her knees. She's breathing hard. The tapping is even louder with the door open, and I see the snowballs actually bouncing when they hit the ground.

"Thank you." Roger hugs her. "I love your snow."

Nevaeh takes two more deep breaths and slowly stands up straight. Her cheeks are pink.

"It's hailstones. Hail is rain that freezes into ice as it comes down," she explains, coming into the house. "I ran over because my father said you might want to put your car in the garage. Hail this big could dent it. He's out there covering Mom's roses."

"Good idea. Thanks. I'll move the car and go help him," Dad says, and heads outside.

Nevaeh and I stand under the porch roof watching the hail come down. Roger runs out onto the lawn and picks up pieces of hail.

"OW, OW!" he yells as the hail comes down on him, but he doesn't go back onto the porch.

"*Hailstones.* Is that one word or two?"

"I think it's one, but I'm not sure."

"See what I mean? It's hard to know," I say.

"I'm really glad you made the rain freeze," Roger calls to Nevaeh.

"What about your dad's truck? Won't the hail dent that, too?" I ask.

"Dad's truck already has dents in it," Nevaeh says as she watches Roger gather the hail. "He knows it's gonna melt, right? It's July."

She picks up a ball of hail. I don't know why she chooses that one—if there's something special about it. She holds it in her hand and studies it, a faraway look on her face.

Even as it starts melting and disappearing off the lawn, Roger is still piling up what's left of the hail and throwing it in the air and, of course, eating it.

And as suddenly as it started, the hail stops. It rains for a few minutes, then the sun comes out, shining on the ground still covered in icy snowballs.

It doesn't surprise me when Nevaeh takes out her pencil and paper. It does surprise me when she finishes writing and passes me her poem without my asking to see it. This one has a title.

Hail in July

If you hadn't seen it yourself
you wouldn't believe I was right.
That the grass was green
and then it turned white.

"I like that. You're a very good writer," I say, and that's when I get the idea to ask her to help me write my own letter to McKenzie. I could explain how sorry Dad is and ask McKenzie to forgive him, so he can forgive himself. It might be harder to write than a weather poem, but I think Nevaeh would have some good ideas about what to say.

Roger's mound of hail gets bigger and bigger.

"I'm gonna put it all in the freezer to show Mommy when she comes," he announces.

While Roger is busy with the hail, I see my chance to talk to Nevaeh about my letter idea.

"I want to show you something," I say, and she follows me inside the house.

Luckily, Dad's letters are short, and Nevaeh is a fast reader. The longer part is telling her why I need help writing my own letter.

"My dad is writing to McKenzie because he was her baby's doctor. He used to take care of very sick babies in the hospital. Some of them were so small he could hold them in one hand. And then he made a mistake when he was taking care of her baby."

"McKenzie's baby died," Nevaeh says. Her bird eyes look down at the cream-colored pages, and I can see her long eyelashes.

"Yes. It wasn't on purpose, but she did die. He's trying to write McKenzie a letter, but this is as far as he's gotten. So I thought I'd write to her myself and explain how sorry he is. And then maybe she'd forgive him, and he could forgive himself. What do you think? Could you help me with the letter?"

"What was the baby's name?" she asks.

"I don't know."

"If you write to McKenzie, you should use the baby's name, not just say *baby*."

"I can't ask Dad but maybe my mom knows. I can find out next time I call her."

Nevaeh looks up at me, and I remember she can't ever call her mother.

"Also, ask if she knows anything else about the baby. How she looked or what she was like. After Mom died, people sent cards to us. Mostly they just said *sorry* or *our sympathies*. The best one was from Campbell's mother. She wrote how Mom used to leave roses in her dooryard every summer and always stuck up for her in school. And that Mom once read her one of my birthday poems."

Before I can answer, Roger comes inside with his hands full of hail. Nevaeh quickly slips the letters back into the desk drawer.

"Mommy is gonna be so surprised, isn't she, Harvard? Don't tell her," he says.

"Don't worry. I won't."

"Come look!" Roger calls from the kitchen a few minutes later.

He's pulled a chair up next to the refrigerator and is standing on it. He waits until we're both there, then opens the freezer door.

Next to packages of frozen corn and ice cube trays, there's a pile of hail.

"Mom will be very surprised," I say, "but if you keep opening the freezer door, all that's going to be there when she comes is one big puddle."

Roger slams the freezer door shut.

"I'm going to collect more," he says, then jumps off the chair and runs back outside.

If Mom comes to Kettle Hole, she'll be surprised to find two jars of honey (one for us and one for the ants), a plate of apple slices turning brown in the refrigerator, and a mountain of hail stacked in the freezer.

Nevaeh is studying the ant farm and waves at me to come over.

"Do you see what's there?" She touches the glass side.

I look more closely.

Tenna is in the hollowed-out room at the end of the tunnel. Underneath her are four tiny oval shapes the color of the hail.

I can't believe my eyes. "Are those . . . ?"

"What else can they be?" Nevaeh says. "Tenna is laying eggs. She's a queen!"

She leans in closer.

"They look like grains of rice all stuck together in the bottom of a bowl."

Sometimes when Nevaeh talks it sounds like she's saying one of her poems.

Roger comes in with another handful of hail.

"Nevaeh, what other weather can you do?"

"There's lots of different kinds of weather, Roger. Sun and rain and wind and snow and hail and—"

"Wind," Roger interrupts. "I pick wind this time. Can you make it really windy? So things blow over?"

"What kind of things?"

"Anything."

"I can try, Roger, but it might take a while."

"That's okay. I'm good at waiting," he says.

I shake my head to show how not true that is, and Nevaeh smiles back.

After he puts the latest collection of hail in the freezer, Roger takes a cooking pot outside with him.

"What's your father going to think about Tenna being a queen?" Nevaeh says.

"I think he's going to like all the little eggs."

We have our faces up close to the ant farm when Dad comes back.

"Is there a problem with the ants?" he asks, and I hear the alarm in his voice.

"No," I say quickly, "we were watching Tenna. Look! She's laying eggs."

Dad's chest heaves like Nevaeh's when she's having trouble breathing.

"This is truly remarkable." His voice comes out in a gasp. He acts as proud and excited as if he'd laid the eggs himself. "I've never heard of a real live queen coming with anyone's ant farm. I should contact the company and inquire about the proper care of a queen."

"NO." I put my hand up like that will stop Dad from contacting the company.

Nevaeh comes to my rescue.

"Mr. Corson, what if someone put a queen in by accident. You wouldn't want them to get in trouble."

I'm glad Nevaeh said *by accident* instead of *by mistake.* I can see the Dad mind-wheels turning.

"You're right, Nevaeh. I wouldn't want someone to lose their job on my account. I'm sure we can read up on the care of queens. It will add a whole new element to our project."

"Great idea, Dad! Let's research it," I say, and scratch my question onto the board.

How do you care for a queen ant?

"I can help research, too," Nevaeh volunteers.

"What's Roger gonna think about Tenna and her eggs?" I say.

Dad clears his throat and looks around the room. Roger is still outside.

Maybe he's remembering what happened when Roger got interested in ant-napping and ant-walking and social stomachs. Is he picturing Roger taking all the eggs in the refrigerator and storing them in a pile in the corner of his room?

The house ants are disappearing one by one in a crack in the ceiling, but they stop in their line when Dad clears his throat.

"No need to distract Roger just yet. He's fully occupied with gathering hail at the moment," he says diplomatically, then carefully covers the ant farm with the dish towel.

FIFTEEN

Hope

I put Dad's emergency flashlight under my bed before I go to sleep, and when I wake up during the night I point its red pulsing light at the jellyfish/sun ceiling cracks.

I quietly close Dad's bedroom door before I head down to check on the ant farm.

Tenna is still in her chamber, and I count eight eggs around her. The worker ants are making a new tunnel on the other side of the ant farm.

I sit at the desk and call Mom. She answers on the third ring.

"Where were you?" I ask.

"I was getting a snack. I had a feeling you'd be calling."

"What kind of snack?"

"A chocolate bar."

"Good choice, Mom," I say.

"How are things going? What have you been doing? Dad says Vern's daughter has been visiting."

"Yes. Her name is Nevaeh. *Ne-vay-ah.*" I sound it out the way Nevaeh did. "She writes poetry."

Instead of answering Mom's other questions, I come right out with my own.

"What was the baby's name?"

There's silence on the phone. Not even the sound of chocolate bar chewing. Then I hear Mom's one word.

"Hope."

This time I'm the one saying nothing on the other end of the phone.

"Harvard, are you still there?"

I pull a sheet of paper out of the desk.

"Hope? H-o-p-e?"

"Yes."

I write down the letters in the baby's name.

I remember what else Nevaeh said to ask.

"What was she like?"

"What do you mean?"

"I don't know. What did she look like? Or what did she do?"

"She was sick, Harvard, so she couldn't do much. She spent her whole life in the hospital. I never met her, but I saw her photo in the paper after she died, and she had a lot of hair for a baby."

I write *LOTS OF HAIR* on the paper below *HOPE*.

We're both quiet for a while, then Mom speaks.

"What else is happening?"

I don't say Roger keeps asking me if I miss her, Roger code for *I miss Mommy*. Or that he thinks Nevaeh is in charge of the weather. I stare at the words *HOPE* and *LOTS OF HAIR*.

"Roger is sharing his food," I finally say.

"That's good to hear. He's always had a generous heart," Mom says, and then yawns.

"Are you done with the chocolate bar?"

"Yes," she laughs, "and I'd better try and get some more sleep. You, too, Harvard. I miss you, my boy. Thanks for having such a great attitude about everything. It's appreciated."

"Good night, Mom," I answer, although I'm not sure what kind of attitude she means. Or what makes it good. The way she says it makes it sound like the whole world appreciates my great attitude.

There are so many things Mom doesn't know about: her son Roger-the-Ant, Tenna-the-Queen, Nevaeh's promises, the hail.

I picture Mom in my parents' bed at home, the big bed we all used to fit in to watch movies. And I remember one of the other things I heard Mom say to Dad after the mistake.

Your guilt is crushing me, Marshall. I can't be in mourning all the time.

How can guilt crush someone? It's not like she's trapped in an avalanche or caught under a building. Now that Dad is in Maine, does she feel like she's floating above the bed, with no weight to hold her down?

I pull open the drawer, and there's a new letter on top of

the others. Is this what Dad does after we fall asleep—sits at the desk and writes letters to McKenzie?

It's the longest one yet, and it's only nine words:

Dear McKenzie,
Not a day goes by that I

It's a good thing Nevaeh is going to help me with my letter to McKenzie, because at this rate, it's going to take Dad a very long time just to finish one sentence.

SIXTEEN

Old Home Day Raffle

I bring my good attitude to breakfast the next morning. Roger is bent over his cereal bowl with his ant helmet on. His antennae touch the cereal before he eats, the way the ants check out their food. The dish towel is still covering the ant farm. Dad is buttering his toast.

I use one of Mom's favorite ways to begin a serious discussion with Dad.

"Marshall, can we talk?"

"Harvard!" Dad stares at me, his forehead all wrinkled, but then I guess he reminds himself about the whole *being a better father* resolution.

"Yes, Harvard." He lowers his voice this time. "What do you want to talk about?"

"Don't you think it's time Roger found some friends here? You know, friends with two legs, not six?"

Roger looks up at me, his wire antennae wobbling back and forth.

"What's wrong with six legs?"

"See what I mean?" I say to Dad.

"I could ask around. Vern probably knows children his age who live around here."

"Nevaeh's my friend." Roger's words are muffled since his face is back in his cereal bowl.

"Wouldn't it be good to have other friends, too? Like today, Nevaeh and I need to work on a special project at her place."

Roger lifts his face out of his food. There's a flake of cereal stuck to his nose.

"I can help."

"It's a surprise," I say, which isn't a lie.

"For me, right?" Roger smiles his missing-tooth grin.

"Not really, Roger. Everything isn't always about you," I say, but I can tell that only makes him more convinced it *is* about him. "When I'm busy, you and your friends could do your own special things. Maybe Dad could take you all to see a movie."

Roger looks up again.

"I could show them the hail," he says, and I imagine Roger and a group of five-year-olds huddled together on a chair staring into the freezer.

I take three sheets of Dad's writing paper, a pencil, two honey sandwiches wrapped in aluminum foil, and *The Natural Genius of Ants* with me. You can't tell the ground was covered in hail yesterday. The grass is as green as ever. I haven't given up on the idea of finding tree treasure, so on the way to Nevaeh's, I tap the trunks of the trees along the path, listening for a hollow sound that might be a clue to a secret compartment.

Nevaeh is outside under the tree with the shaggy bark. I smell a whiff of cigarette smoke in the air. A cloth headband with horses on it holds back her hair.

"Paper and brain food," I say, showing her what I brought. "And don't worry, there's no grease or termites or insect parts in the sandwiches."

"Good, because I don't eat meat," she answers.

I make a surprised face. I didn't know that about her.

"And neither do horses," she adds.

"Plus the book, so we can look up about the care of queen ants."

When we go inside, Nevaeh makes room on the table, pushing aside two flyswatters and pieces of screening. I hear hammering sounds from the side of the barn.

"Dad's outside on a ladder fixing the screen in my loft. It fell out of the window during the night and the place filled up with mosquitoes."

It's true. There's a whining noise around my head, and mosquitoes land on my arms and the back of my neck. Nevaeh slaps at the ones around her.

I give her the paper I wrote on when I was talking to Mom and explain what *HOPE* and *LOTS OF HAIR* mean.

"How should I start?" I ask. "*Dear McKenzie*, right? And then what?"

"Write *Dear McKenzie* and then wait and see what you think of next."

"Is that how you do it with the poems?" I ask.

She shrugs and unwraps one of the honey sandwiches. I unwrap and bite into the other sandwich. While we eat, Nevaeh opens *The Natural Genius of Ants* to the middle, where the photographs are, and turns the book so we can both see the pictures of queen ants and their eggs.

Maybe honey sandwiches are brain food, because once I finish my sandwich and pick up the pencil to start writing, all the words come rushing out.

Dear McKenzie,

I'm writing about your baby Hope.

My father (Dr. Corson) wrote you four letters but he didn't finish the first sentence in any of the letters. If you read them, you would see how sorry he is about your baby.

I never met Hope, but my Mom saw her picture in the paper and said she had a lot of hair. And that she was in the hospital a long time. I'm really sorry she died.

My dad will never forget Hope. He thinks about her all the time. Now that he stopped being a doctor, all he has to take care of is our ants.

Can you forgive him?

If you can, maybe he could forgive himself and
be happy again.

Yours truly,
Harvard Corson (son of Dr. Corson)
age 10

Nevaeh reads the letter slowly, one finger stopping on
some of the lines.

"It's great," she finally says, "especially the part about
Hope's hair. But you might want to take out the ant part
because it's not really true. Your father doesn't just have the
ants to take care of. He has you and Roger."

Nevaeh is a poet and a better writer than I am, but I don't
want to take out the ant part. If McKenzie could see how
Dad is with the ants, she would understand how much he
misses the babies he used to take care of.

So I erase that sentence and change it to:

Now that he stopped being a doctor, all
he has to take care of is me and my younger
brother Roger and an ant farm.

"Do you know where to mail it? You'll need McKenzie's
last name and address. If you knew her last name, you could
look it up. My mom's obituary has her photo and what town
she lived in."

Nevaeh opens a drawer in front of her in the wooden

kitchen table and hands me a newspaper clipping. At the top it says:

Earlene Redlevske Knowles

There's a photo of a woman with eyes like Nevaeh's. She's looking straight ahead, and I think she's on the porch of the house. In the obituary it says she was married to Vernon Knowles, had one daughter, Nevaeh, and lived in Kettle Hole, Maine. It also says she grew roses.

I shake my head. I didn't think that far ahead.

"I can't use Dad's cell phone to look it up. Anyway, I don't even know her last name."

Nevaeh puts the obituary back in the drawer and picks up one of the flyswatters. Swat. Swat. Swat. She kills three mosquitoes in a row, smashing the last one on a calendar nailed to the wall. The nail and the calendar both fall to the floor. The calendar opens to August, and I notice August 9th is circled in red and says *OLD HOME DAY* in capital letters.

"Old Home Day?" I ask.

"Are you going?" Nevaeh's face lights up with a big smile. "Your father should definitely go, since he grew up here."

"What's Old Home Day?"

"It's the best time! Even better than the Fourth of July, especially since the town stopped having fireworks. There's a dinner, a craft fair, and a talent show. Plus a raffle and a parade and a footrace. And last year they had a corn-eating contest. People who grew up in Kettle Hole and moved away come back and meet each other. That's why it's called Old Home Day. It's like a birthday for the town and the people who live here and used to live here."

"Do you go in the parade?" I ask.

"No, I never have, but I watch it."

"What about the talent show?"

"I can't sing or whistle or dance or play an instrument."

"The footrace?"

"No. Running makes me cough."

"Corn-eating contest?"

"You have to eat a lot of corn to win."

"What about the raffle?"

"I buy a ticket, but I've never won yet."

"What kind of raffle?"

"It's different every year. Last year the raffle prize was a quilt. You paid a dollar and guessed how many gumdrops were in a big jar. And the one who guessed closest won the quilt."

"Are there going to be a lot of kids there?"

"Yes, most all the kids in Kettle Hole go."

That's when I get my brilliant idea to help Nevaeh with her mother's second promise—to find a friend who can read her mind.

"Can we have our own raffle?" I ask, then continue, "Everyone would have to guess a word you thought up, and whoever guessed it right would be the friend your mom was thinking of. We could have it be a free raffle, so more kids would enter. The only thing is we'd need a prize."

My Harvard mind-wheels start turning, and I think of the perfect prize.

"The prize could be a poem. Whoever wins, you could write them a poem. A poem *about* them."

I pick up a flyswatter from the table and speak into it like it's a microphone, waving my other arm toward myself as if there's a big crowd around us in the barn house.

"Step right up. Guess the secret word and win a poem by a genuine Kettle Hole poet! Free guesses for everyone!"

Nevaeh doesn't look excited about my idea.

"That's not how it works with poetry."

"It doesn't have to be long. Here's one." I think for a minute, then speak into the flyswatter again.

"She controls the rain and snow

Roger hopes she makes wind blow.

Her name reminds me of a place called heaven,

and she can herd as many ants as seven."

Nevaeh giggles.

"It's the first poem I ever wrote. What do you say? Isn't that a good prize? Who wouldn't want a poem about themself?"

Nevaeh looks around the room.

"Well, I don't have anything else to give for a prize. I'll call Campbell's mom and see if we can have a raffle table. She's head of the Old Home Day Committee. And I have an empty fishbowl we can put the guesses in."

"What's your secret word going to be?" I ask her.

"I already know what it is, but it wouldn't be a secret if I told you," she says.

SEVENTEEN

Nodrog Spelled Backwards

With Old Home Day coming, we're all suddenly very busy.

Dad takes my good-attitude advice about finding Roger a friend. He calls people he hasn't seen in years and makes a list titled *Playdates.* On Monday, Wednesday, and Friday, Dad invites a different Kettle Hole kid to the house.

Monday is Leland. He calls Roger's hail *lumpy ice cubes* and says the ant farm smells weird. Wednesday is Iris. I'm out riding my bike during the playdate, but I hear about it afterward. Iris accidentally pulls one of Roger's antennae off his helmet. He cries so hard he throws up on the floor and Iris demands to be taken home immediately.

Friday is Gordon. His grandmother brings him over, and

Dad goes out to say hi to her. Gordon is like the Tenna of little boys—a head taller and bigger than Roger. His head is shaved and Gordon points to it.

"My grandma shaved my head. We all had lice. My brother brought them back from music camp."

He makes crawly motions with his fingers on top of his head. "Lice are bugs who like to live in hair."

"Wow," Roger says, staring at him. "We don't have lice, but we have ants. Do you want to see them?"

Roger and Gordon hit it off right away. Nodrog spelled backwards tells Roger he'll collect hail for him if any falls at his place. They go outside and spend all morning literally running around and around the house. I see Gordon's bald head whish past the windows, Roger's following behind.

When they finally come in, Roger explains why we have a blackboard on the wall in our living room and generously offers Gordon a piece of chalk. I watch while Gordon writes, sure there's going to be a question like DO ANS PI AND PUP? Under my care-of-a-queen question, Gordon writes, with perfect spelling:

DO ANTS BITE?

"Great question, Gordon." Roger compliments his new friend.

"Thank you. I thought of another question, too. Do ants talk?"

Then Gordon proceeds to speak the way he thinks ants talk. It sounds like this:

Eek Eek Eeka Leeka Uh Oh Eeka

Roger is a fast learner and talks back to him.

Oo-ee Oo-eek Gre Gre

This keeps both boys laughing for the next five minutes.

Campbell's mother gives Nevaeh the go-ahead for the poetry raffle, and we make posters. Mine has each letter in a different color and says:

READ HER MIND
GUESS THE WORD
WIN A POEM
ALL ABOUT YOU

Nevaeh is as good at drawing as she is at poems, and her drawing of a bowl full of paper guesses looks like a real one. She even draws an orange goldfish with fins and a boomerang-shaped tail swimming through the papers, like it's trying to find the one with the right answer.

There are twelve eggs in the room at the end of the

tunnel. Tenna hasn't laid any new eggs in two days. The tunnel on the other side of the ant farm is almost four inches long, and the worker ants go back and forth carrying out the dirt. I watch them pile it up on top of the ant farm, making little hills.

Roger eventually notices the eggs under Tenna, but they don't interest him the way I thought they would.

"They're cool, aren't they? They're real ant eggs," I say.

Roger watches the tiny eggs for a few minutes.

"Nothing's happening," he finally says.

"Not yet, but it will. One day new ants will hatch, and they'll be her workers. They'll find food for her and make the tunnels and clean up."

"If I make more new friends, some of them could be my workers."

"That's not what friends are for, Roger," I point out, but he stares ahead, as if he's imagining a bunch of little kids bringing him snacks and cleaning his room.

The blackboard question about care of a queen was easy to answer.

Nevaeh and I read about queen ants, and it turns out the care of a queen comes down to one word. Nothing. Gnihton. Queens already have everything they need. Food stored in their private stomach, enough eggs in their bodies for a lifetime, and workers to do everything else.

Roger is so worn out from running with Gordon he leans on one elbow, studying the ant farm and yawning during supper.

"Gordon invited me to his house on Monday to swim in his pool," he tells Dad, then adds, "and he has lice."

Dad, who missed that part of Gordon's introduction, takes the pen out of his shirt pocket and writes something on the bottom of the playdate list.

"Look. Those two ants are still napping upside down. They must be tired," Roger comments, but I'm thinking about the raffle and don't pay much attention to my brother's observation. Dad is distracted, too, probably thinking about Gordon's lice, and neither of us bother to look where Roger is pointing to see what's happening in the ant farm.

EIGHTEEN

Dad's Letter

The evening of Gordon's visit, Roger falls asleep when it's still light out, without a word of the ice fishing story. Something keeps nagging at me about his comment at dinner—*Those two ants are still napping upside down*—and I go check on the ant farm.

Dad is sitting at the desk with his pen suspended over the paper. This surprises me, as I've never seen him write any of his letters to McKenzie before.

"What are you writing?" I ask, like I don't know about all the unfinished sentences.

"I'm trying to write a letter." Dad sighs.

I give Dad a pep talk.

"Nevaeh is a really good writer. I've seen her write poems.

When she starts she gets this concentrated look on her face, and she doesn't put down her pencil until she's all done."

I pretend-scribble very fast with my hand in the air, poking one finger out to do the period at the end of the sentences. I jump around while I'm doing it to make it look fun.

Dad watches my demonstration and seems to think about my writing tips.

"That might be the way to do it," he agrees.

"Good job on finding a friend for Roger, Dad."

"Thank you, Harvard. In fact, we may be up to two friends. Iris's father called and invited Roger to their house. He said Iris felt bad about how the last playdate ended. And Roger is eager to go."

"Great news! Why let an accidental antenna injury interfere with a potential friendship?"

"Don't leave the ant farm uncovered too long," Dad says when he sees me go over to the kitchen table. "I read it's important to give a new queen and her eggs as much privacy and darkness as possible."

Dad talked like this about the preemie babies who were born way too early. In order to make them feel like they were still inside their mothers, the doctors and nurses kept the lights dim and covered the tops of their plastic boxes with a blanket.

"Okay," I say.

Dad goes back to his letter. He might be taking my advice, because he's biting his bottom lip and his pen is moving across the paper. The house ants make circles around Dad's chair, like they're also excited to see him writing.

I take that as my second good-attitude win, the first getting Dad to find Roger almost two friends.

When I uncover the ant farm, what I see makes me think of another thing Dad used to say about his work, which never made much sense to me until now.

It's so easy not to see something if you're convinced you know what's going on.

I thought the most important thing happening in the ant farm was Tenna and her eggs and missed seeing what Roger noticed. Along the walls of the longer tunnel, two ants lie without moving, their legs and antennae stiff. One is on its back with its legs out, and the other is partway on its side. Other ants walk right over them, not in a mean way, but as if they're part of the tunnel floor. From my experience with the not-live ants that were shipped in the tube, I can tell these upside-down and sideways ants are definitely dead.

I sigh like Dad did. I can't help it. I didn't know the ants were sick, and now they're dead.

I'm realizing how hard it is to keep things alive. Especially ants. Why did I pick ants? I could have said I wanted to study big turtles. Some of them live longer than people. Or parrots. My friend Tobias's parents have a parrot that's forty years old. And it talks, too.

The ants are like Dad's babies. They can't say they're not feeling well or where it hurts. Maybe ants can tell another ant, but then what can that ant do? There's no ant hospital.

"Done," I hear Dad exclaim, and when I look over, he's pressing down the flap of an envelope to seal it. "Thanks for the useful suggestion about Nevaeh's poetry-writing techniques. And how are things in the ant world? Has our resident queen laid any more eggs?"

Dad sounds pleased with himself, almost cheerful, and I can't bring myself to say what else is happening in the ant farm. If he discovers the ant farm ants are dying, will all the cheerfulness disappear?

I do a quick count.

"There's fourteen eggs now," I report. I go over to where Dad is sitting at the desk. He puts on a stamp and holds up the cream-colored envelope. That's when I see the name and address written on the front.

It's not McKenzie's name there. It is Mom's name and our address six states away.

Dad puts the letter down but keeps a hand on it.

"When your Mom and I were first dating and had to be apart, we'd write each other letters. Once I started, I found I had more to say than I thought. I told Mom about the successful playdate with Gordon and suggested we get Roger a weather radio for his birthday. He seems to have developed quite an interest in the weather."

I try not to show my disappointment. I didn't magically get Dad to finish a letter to McKenzie. I search for something to say that doesn't have to do with letters, mistakes, or the ant farm.

"Are you going to Old Home Day? It's on August ninth. I'm helping Nevaeh with a raffle."

"Old Home Day! Of course! I don't want to miss that." His face lights up the same way Nevaeh's did.

"How come you never came back for Old Home Day

before? Nevaeh says that's what the day is for, people who lived here coming back and seeing each other."

"I thought about coming many years, but there never seemed to be a good time to make the trip."

"Well, you don't have to make a trip this year. You're already here."

"I certainly am," Dad says.

"Could I keep the ant farm in my room, just for tonight?" I ask. I can't think of any other way of keeping him from noticing the dead ants. This would give me time to figure out a plan.

"I want to do some research," I add, and point to the blackboard where Gordon's question is written in yellow chalk. I don't say the research I need to do is about dead ants or that Nevaeh still has *The Natural Genius of Ants* book at the barn house.

Dad looks up at the blackboard and raises his eyebrows.

"Sure," he says distractedly, and goes back to gazing at the cream-colored envelope like it's Mom herself in front of him.

NINETEEN

Ant Graveyard

The first thing I do when I wake up is take the dish towel off the ant farm. My mouth opens so wide that if I was at Nevaeh's house, a mosquito could have flown in and bit my tonsils.

One of the dead ants is being dragged and pushed out of the tunnel. Two ants are pushing the dead ant with their heads, and another ant is pulling it with its front legs. In a corner of the ant farm the other dead ant is lying on its side. The worker ants drop bits of dirt over the dead ants, and I realize I'm looking at an ant graveyard.

There's a third ant that's not looking so good. It's moving very, very slowly, and sometimes it stops the way Nevaeh does when she tries to catch her breath.

I cover the ant farm and climb out the window. I need to get Nevaeh's help before Dad finds out what's happening.

I'm across the roof, down the arbor, up the path, and knocking on the barn house door in record time.

I was counting on talking to Nevaeh alone, but Campbell opens the door.

She isn't bouncing a ball like last time, but she's running in place like she's on an imaginary treadmill. She is wearing a different striped shirt than last time—these stripes are purple and gray. The purple is the same color as her glasses.

I figure I have bigger worries than Campbell knowing about the dead ants.

I clear my throat like Dad before I speak.

"Ants are dying in the ant farm. Two already died and one looks sick. The workers are taking them to some kind of ant graveyard and covering them with dirt."

Nevaeh and Campbell have completely different reactions. Nevaeh gets teary-eyed and sniffs like Roger before he cries. Campbell bursts out laughing like it's the funniest thing she's ever heard. She stops running in place and holds both her hands over her stomach to show how funny she thinks it is.

"An ant graveyard? You gonna have an ant funeral? You gonna have an ant minister give a speech? You gonna have an ant gravestone? You gonna—"

"Campbell!" Nevaeh gently pokes her sneaker against Campbell's. "Harvard cares about the ants, and so do I. They're living things."

Campbell straightens up.

"So are the mosquitoes in here, but you still kill them," she says.

"My father cares about the ants, too," I explain to Campbell, who does have a point about the mosquitoes. "He'll be upset if he finds out they died."

Campbell gives me a strange look.

"He killed a baby and he's going to freak out about an ant?"

"Campbell!" Nevaeh raises her voice. "You don't know the whole story."

I'm glad Nevaeh didn't say, *Everybody makes mistakes.*

"My mother says it's true."

"He didn't kill anyone on purpose," I say quickly. "He's a good doctor. It was a mistake. And now he can't forgive himself. If he finds out ants are dying, it'll be another thing he blames himself for."

Don't make the same mistake twice.

Campbell pushes her purple glasses up on her nose.

"Maybe they were old ants? Like grandmother and grandfather ants. Ants don't live forever, right?" she says.

"I didn't think of that," I admit. "I don't know how to tell if an ant is old."

"Do they walk really slow? Like this?"

Campbell gets on the floor and starts crawling in slow motion.

"You need to meet my brother, Roger," I tell Campbell. "You two would get along really well."

"Is he cute?" Campbell asks.

"Very."

"It's only two, maybe three ants," Nevaeh says. "Does your father count them every day?"

"No, the only thing he's been counting is Tenna's eggs."

"Who's Tenna?" Campbell asks.

"Tenna is the queen."

"Couldn't we add a little dirt to the graveyard so he doesn't see the dead ants? It would be like helping the workers," Nevaeh suggests. "And then we can wait and see if any more ants die."

I knew Nevaeh would have a good idea.

"Okay. Can you come over now?"

"I want to see this ant graveyard, too," Campbell says.

"And I need to borrow back the ant book." I take *The Natural Genius of Ants* off the table. "Roger's new friend Gordon wrote a question on the blackboard."

There's a photo sticking out of the top of the book. It's a horse, and its head is turned like it's looking at something.

"I was using it as a bookmark," Nevaeh says. "Joker was watching me, probably hoping I brought him an apple."

I turn it over, and there are words in Nevaeh's small printing.

Brown all over
except a white teardrop-shaped mark
on his forehead.
Shy of sticks
afraid of the sound of chickens clucking,
but otherwise fearless.

Answers to the name of
Joker.

"It's a photo bookmark poem," I say, and give it back to
her. Nevaeh puts it away in the same table drawer she took
her mother's obituary from. Campbell does three jumping
jacks in a row. Then we all head over to see the ant graveyard.

TWENTY

Twenty-Three Miles

I guess there's a reason they're called *worker* ants. And it's no wonder they have to take so many naps. In the time it took me to go to Nevaeh's and back, the workers have moved the second dead ant near the first one in the ant graveyard, and she's already half covered in dirt.

The sick-looking ant is moving as slowly as Campbell did when she pretended to be an old ant.

In Tenna's tunnel there's more activity than ever. Worker ants gather around the eggs and it looks like they're dusting them with their front legs and kissing or licking them with their mouths. One worker ant picks up an egg in her mouth, moves it an inch, and puts it back down. Another worker ant sticks an egg to the ceiling of the tunnel.

On the way over Nevaeh grabbed a handful of dark-colored dirt from under the rosebushes next to the barn. She opens the ant farm cover and gently sprinkles the dirt until both dead ants are covered. If you didn't know where to look, you wouldn't notice the little bit of shiny black ant leg showing through in one place.

Campbell stretches out on the rug in my room.

I hear Roger climb the stairs, jumping past steps two and nine.

He looks down at Campbell. "Hi, I'm Roger. I'm five."

"Cool! I'm Campbell. I'm eleven."

"Nevaeh does the weather. What can you do?"

This is Roger for *What can you do for me?*

"I can run," Campbell says.

"That's easy. So can I. My friend Gordon and I ran all around the house. Like this." And Roger runs in a circle around her.

"I'm training because one day I want to run all the roads in Kettle Hole. The town report says there's twenty-three miles of roads."

"Can I run with you?" Roger asks.

I'm pretty sure he has no idea how far twenty-three miles is.

"If you want," Campbell says. "Or you could man a water station for me along the route."

Now I'm thinking Campbell has no idea how Dad would react to the idea of Roger waiting for her out on the road with a cup of water.

When Dad comes in, there are five people in my room.

I like the way it feels. With Mom not here we are minus one. With Campbell and Nevaeh and Dad and Roger and me we're plus one. Do the ants notice when other ants are missing? They're minus two, almost three now, but when Tenna's daughters hatch they'll be plus fourteen.

"This is Campbell. She can run." Roger introduces Dad to Campbell.

Campbell waves to Dad from her spot on the rug.

"My mom was in your class. Yvonne Billings. She says you were Kettle Hole High's class valedictorian. You must have studied a lot."

"I did. I remember watching your mom in the school cross-country races. You tell her I said hi."

Then Dad takes Roger's hand and turns to me. "I'm taking Roger over to Iris's. We'll be back later."

"Don't forget to look at our blackboard, everyone," Roger reminds us on his way out. "My new friend Gordon wrote an ant question."

When they leave, Campbell says, "Your father is nice. If he met someone who did something worse than he did, do you think he'd forgive himself?"

"I don't know. Maybe."

Campbell starts doing sit-ups with her hands behind her head—one, two, three, four—as she talks.

"Our next-door neighbor Mr. Tracy burned his own house down by mistake frying doughnuts. It took four fire trucks to put it out. And his brother Wallace Tracy once cut a tree on his back lawn, and it went the wrong way and crashed into his glass greenhouse. My mother says the Tracy brothers have the worst luck. Then there's Mary Worth, who brought a blueberry pie to the Old Home Day supper, only she took wild grapes out of her freezer instead of blueberries and my father broke a tooth on the seeds. Or he could talk to Mrs. Sidelinger. She left her son in the car in his car seat. She thought she dropped him at day care, but she forgot. It was summer and he got too hot and died. My mother says she could never survive something like that."

A chill goes through my body when I hear about Mrs. Sidelinger. A burnt house and a broken tooth aren't good, but if anyone can understand Dad it would be Mrs. Sidelinger.

"Your mother says a lot of things," I comment.

A laugh comes out of Nevaeh's mouth before she can stop it. I know because that's how it happens with me.

"Good job hiding the dead ants, Nevaeh. Dad didn't notice a thing."

Campbell suddenly jumps up from the floor.

"What's on this blackboard of yours?" she asks.

The way Campbell moves reminds me of a red fox I saw in the tall grass at the edge of the lawn. It walked very slowly, then stood completely still for the longest time. I was just about to give up watching when it pounced on something I couldn't see.

And I wonder how long it would take to run twenty-three miles and what it would be like to see every mile of every road in Kettle Hole.

TWENTY-ONE

Running Out of Time

In the middle of the night, I turn on the lamp and watch the house ants crawling under the desk while I wait for Mom to answer her phone.

"Hi, Harvard, so good to hear your voice. I'm just up making myself some hot milk."

Mom used to make me hot milk when I couldn't sleep.

"Were you having trouble sleeping?"

"I guess I was. How are things there?"

What would Mom say if I told her two ants were dead and one was in critical condition? That I met a girl who wants to run every road in Kettle Hole? That Nevaeh's house filled up with mosquitoes and a letter from Dad in a cream-colored envelope was on its way to her?

"Roger has a special surprise for you in the freezer when you come."

"It's fun that he and Dad are baking together."

Mom must be thinking of cupcakes or cookies frozen for her when she visits.

"Don't get your hopes up," I warn her.

"I won't."

I hear Mom sip her milk.

"How are you? Dad says you're enjoying the ant farm."

I don't think the word *enjoying* is how I'd describe things right now, but I give her my best good-attitude answer.

"The queen is laying eggs to make more workers. The worker ants are all female and they do everything. They take care of the eggs and make the tunnels and search for food and defend the nest and even take out the trash."

Taking out the trash was one of my jobs back home, but I took it down an elevator instead of through a tunnel.

"Really? I guess everyone does what they can," she says, then yawns, as if all my talk about working makes her tired. And I don't know if she means that it's ants or humans who do what they can.

"Are you coming for Old Home Day? It's like a celebration of Kettle Hole. There's a dinner and a parade and a fair. It's on August ninth and I'm helping Nevaeh with a raffle."

"That sounds wonderful!" Mom says. "I've been trying to figure out the best time to come. I'll put it on my calendar and ask for the days off."

While we're talking, I open the desk drawer. There's one new letter.

Dear McKenzie,
Every morning and every night

Dad is back to a seven-word unfinished sentence. He's not making any progress with his letters. If Mom comes for Old Home Day, I'm running out of time for her to see that Dad has forgiven himself, so she doesn't have to be weighed down by his guilt. I have less than a month to find McKenzie's address and talk to Mrs. Sidelinger. I stare at the blackboard across the living room. Under Gordon's question is my latest one.

Which came first—the queen or the eggs?

"Harvard, are you still there?" Mom asks.

"Yes," I say, but I'm distracted during the rest of the phone call.

When we hang up, I close the desk drawer, but it won't shut all the way, like something is stuck in the back. So I give it a harder push to slam it closed. Then I feel a bite on my right ankle. It's sharper than a deerfly bite, and it really hurts.

"Ouch," I can't help saying out loud.

I feel another pinch and look down at my legs. Pinch. Bite. Pinch. Bite. The house ants are biting my ankles. There's the answer to Gordon's blackboard question. Yes. Ants do bite. I pull my legs back, and on the floor under the desk is a cream-colored envelope with one letter written on the outside of it.

H.

The envelope isn't sealed. Inside is a newspaper clipping with a photo of a baby's face, and the baby has a lot of hair.

The house ants drop off my ankles and go back in their line, as if they never attacked me in the first place.

At the bottom of the obituary for baby Hope, the last sentence says:

A celebration of life for our daughter Hope will be held at our house on Sunday, January 26, at 1345 Green Street.

And there it is—the address six states away to send my letter to McKenzie.

TWENTY-TWO

Kettle Hole Pond

The morning after Nevaeh covered the dead ants in the graveyard and Campbell told me about Mrs. Sidelinger, I can't find the sick ant anywhere in the ant farm. I don't know if it got better or if it already died and is buried with the others. I hope it's recovered and back to digging tunnels and eating honey.

Roger is at Gordon's house, and Dad is writing on the blackboard.

"How are things looking in the ant farm?" he asks.

"Fine," I say.

It's almost impossible to count ants in an ant farm, which is good, because then Dad won't notice if it's short a few ants.

Once I reached in to move the bark and five ants ran out from under it. There's no way to know where all the ants are hiding without taking everything apart.

I remember one thing the not-live-ant pamphlet said:

**It's good to vary the diet of your ants.
You could give them an occasional treat
of a fly or a cricket.**

Maybe flies and crickets are like vitamins for ants, and that's why they're getting sick. They could be vitamin deficient. No vitamin C (cricket) or vitamin F (fly) in their diet. There are clusters of dead flies in the kitchen windowsill over the sink. I drop in two vitamin Fs—one on each side of the ant farm.

"What are you writing about, Dad?" I ask.

"Take a look. We have a unique opportunity to study the transformation of eggs into ants, so I thought we should be prepared to understand what we're observing."

I read what he's written, all in capital letters.

METAMORPHOSIS

Underneath is written:

EGG LARVA PUPA ADULT

"Wow, I hope you don't expect Roger to be able to spell *metamorphosis*. That's pretty advanced for a first grader."

Dad looks at me with the same focus he gave to writing on the blackboard.

"How are things going this summer, Harvard? Are you liking it here in Kettle Hole? Do you need more friends? Should we invite one of your friends from home to visit?"

I picture a piece of paper with *Harvard's Playdates* written at the top.

"Tobias is visiting his grandparents in the Philippines for the summer," I say. "But I'm fine. I like it here. Don't you? It's where you grew up. We learned in school how turtles return to the exact same beach where they were born to lay their own eggs. And so do salmon and sharks and seals. Not that you are going to lay eggs, obviously. But Kettle Hole is like your home beach, isn't it?"

"Yes. I think it is," he says.

"It's like how Abuela keeps going back to Santo Domingo. I want to go there, too, sometime. We should all go. Only don't pack too many snacks for Roger to eat on the plane."

"I can talk to Mom about it," Dad says.

"I told Mom about Old Home Day. She's going to come."

"Yes, she texted me about that," Dad says, turning his head toward the front window, as if she might come down the driveway at any minute. I felt the same way when I first heard the UPS truck coming down the driveway with the ant delivery, before I looked out the window. I thought maybe it was Mom coming for a surprise visit.

My letter to McKenzie is in my backpack, and Nevaeh and I are going to ride to the post office to mail it. On the way back we'll stop at Mrs. Sidelinger's house. She doesn't know we're coming, but I'm hoping she's home.

"By the way, Nevaeh and I are taking a bike ride today."

"Sure, don't forget to wear your helmet," he says, and starts drawing on the blackboard. Under **EGG** he draws an oval the shape of Tenna's eggs and colors it in with the white chalk. Under **LARVA** he draws what looks like a long banana, bigger than the egg, colors it white, too, and makes lines sticking out all over it.

"What are the lines?" I ask.

"Little sticky hairs," he answers.

"The larvae are hairy?"

"Yes."

Then he takes the blue chalk and draws a circle in the top of the hairy larva banana.

"What's that?"

"The mouth. Larvae don't have eyes, but they have a mouth."

Dad steps back to examine the hairy, eyeless larvae.

"What do they eat?" I ask.

"The worker ants feed them from their social stomachs," Dad says. He turns and faces me, holding up a finger. "But let's keep that fact between the two of us."

I pull a pretend zipper across my mouth.

"How long does it take for the eggs to go from larvae to pupae to ants?" I ask, expecting Dad to tell me where I can look it up.

"Between four and six weeks."

I do the math in my head.

"So it's possible they'll hatch by Old Home Day."

"It's possible," Dad says. "It's very possible."

"Good coloring, Dad! See you later," I say, picking up my backpack and heading out the door. I'm curious to see what **PUPA** looks like, but I've got things to do.

When I come into the maple grove I bend my head back and try to look as high up into the Don't Cut 'Em trees as I can. I haven't given up on finding the treasure, if it's there.

I'm walking with my head so far back I almost run into Mr. Knowles's truck idling in the yard. Nevaeh is helping him load his shoeing tools into the bed.

"Emergency shoeing call," she says. "Want to come with us?"

"Okay. What's the emergency?"

"A woman called about her horse that threw a shoe. Dad's never been there before. Her regular farrier is on vacation."

"How far did the horse throw it?" I ask. I pull off my sneaker, wind up, and throw as hard as I can. "This far?"

Nevaeh and Mr. Knowles laugh.

"Throwing a shoe means one of the horse's shoes came off," Nevaeh says. "Dad has to nail it back on."

I hop on one foot toward the woods where my sneaker landed, pick make-believe nails out from between my lips, and use an imaginary hammer to pretend nail my sneaker back on.

"I have to run and tell Dad I'm going with you. And can we stop at the post office on the way?"

"That we can!" Mr. Knowles says.

A bell that hangs on the post office door rings when I open it. At first, there's no one there, but then a man comes out of a back room. He has wire-rimmed eyeglasses and his hair is all white. He sits behind the counter on a high stool, takes my money, and looks at the cream-colored letters to McKenzie and Tobias. I wrote one to Tobias last night, in case he gets back home before I do.

He reads my name out loud, "Harvard Corson. Are you related to the Harvard Corson from Kettle Hole?"

"*I'M* Harvard Corson. And my father is Marshall Corson," I say.

The man studies me.

"Then we've met before," he says.

"I don't THINK so . . ." I say.

"You're Harvard Corson's great-grandson. I saw you at his funeral. You were just a baby. Harvard was a good friend and neighbor."

So this is not the first time I've been to Kettle Hole. No one told me that.

"Did you go ice fishing with my grandfather?" I ask.

"Yes, I did. I could tell you some stories."

I'm afraid the man is going to start telling me the ice fishing stories right now. I look over my shoulder where Nevaeh and Mr. Knowles are waiting in the truck. I wave and Nevaeh waves back. I know I'm making them late to the emergency shoeing call.

"Can I come hear them another time? My friend's father is waiting." I point out to the truck by the curb.

"I saw Mr. Knowles brought you. You're welcome

anytime. I'm here every day except Saturday afternoons and Sundays," he says.

The bell on the door rings again when I open it to leave.

Mr. Knowles's truck continues down the dirt road. It hasn't rained since the day it hailed, and as we drive the dust blows up around the car. I look through the back window and see the clouds of dust still hanging in the air.

"I thought we'd make a quick detour, show you where Kettle Hole got its name." Mr. Knowles drives the same way as last time—one hand on the wheel and the other hanging out his open window. Dad always drives with both hands on the wheel.

"I thought it was an emergency," I say. If Dad got called for a hospital emergency when we were in the middle of supper, he wouldn't even finish his meal.

"It's mostly on the way," Mr. Knowles says, then hums to himself as the truck continues down the dusty roads.

Nevaeh pokes me with her elbow and points out the window.

I get a quick glance of a yellow house through the hanging-down branches of a tree in the front yard.

"Mrs. Sidelinger's house," she whispers. "The one with the weeping willow."

Finally, Mr. Knowles pulls off on the side of the road. There are woods all around us. We get out of the truck, and he leads the way down a path I couldn't even tell was there. We walk downhill until we come to a clearing.

"Here it is," Mr. Knowles says.

He stands at the edge of a huge crater. It's perfectly round and filled with water.

I expected a hole like the potholes in city streets, or a hole someone dug with a shovel, with dirt all around it. This is bigger than anything I imagined. The water is greenish blue, and you can see the reflections of clouds in it.

"Here you have it. A kettle hole pond," Mr. Knowles says. "Courtesy of a glacier."

"A glacier made it? How did it do that?"

"The hole was full of buried ice. After the glacier left, it melted."

"How deep is it?"

Mr. Knowles bends down and dips his hands in the water.

"Stories about this pond go way back. Some people say it's bottomless and other people swear they touched bottom and it was hard as rock. One story has it if you swim in here, you'll always return to Kettle Hole. As kids, we were warned to stay away because the sides are so steep. They said if you went in, you might not be able to climb out. Of course that made me want to go in all the more."

"Tell Harvard what you and Mr. Corson did," Nevaeh says.

"Oh, yes, that adventure! Marshall didn't want any part of it, but I talked him into coming with me. Before we left, he went out to the shed and came back with the longest rope he could find. I jumped from up there." Mr. Knowles points to a place on the other side of the pond. "Going in was easy, but the stories were true. Getting out was tricky. The sides were slippery, all wet with mud. That rope of your father's came in mighty handy."

"I know what I'd do," I say. "I'd jump in the kettle hole pond. What would you do, Nevaeh? Jump in or wait with a rope."

"I don't know," she says. "I guess it would depend on the day."

"You could sit on the edge and write a poem about it," I suggest.

"Maybe I would," she says.

On the uphill walk back, Nevaeh is last in line. She stops a few times, coughing, and I wait for her to catch up. She takes the red inhaler from her pocket and squeezes out a puff.

As we drive along some of the twenty-three miles of Kettle Hole roads to the emergency shoeing call, I hang one arm out my open window and wonder what Nevaeh would write about the possibly bottomless circle of water that gave the town its name.

TWENTY-THREE

Cow-Kicked

Mr. Knowles pulls up in front of a fenced-in field and a sign that reads:

SECOND CHANCES HORSE HAVEN

"C'mon, Harvard, let's go over to the pasture." Nevaeh is practically out the door before the truck stops.

We walk along the fence. They all look like horses to me, but to Nevaeh each one is different.

"There's an Arabian, that's a mini-horse, and see the sweet Shetland pony? Oh, and the horse over there is underweight, poor boy, look at his ribs," she says.

Then she stops and watches a horse that's mostly white with brown splotches on its sides. The sun is bright in our faces, and she cups her hands over her eyes.

"Something's wrong with that horse."

"How do you know?" I ask.

"See how her ears are pinned back. And the look in her eyes."

"What look?"

Suddenly the white-and-brown-colored horse turns, bares her teeth, and bites the Shetland pony on the neck. The pony runs off. It's over so quickly I'm not sure exactly what happened.

"Did you see that?" Nevaeh says.

"Yeah. Why did she bite the other horse? What did it do?"

"It didn't do anything."

"That's mean."

We continue walking along the fence until a woman comes out of a barn at the end of the driveway. She's wearing a straw sun hat and carrying a pink-and-purple rope. She walks across the field and goes over to the biter horse. When she gets closer I see her shirt also says SECOND CHANCES HORSE HAVEN.

"Zellie, sweet girl," she says to the horse, hooking the rope to her halter. I know it's called a halter because Nevaeh told me what it was when we saw Frontier Ben.

"Oh, no," Nevaeh says under her breath. "I just noticed. She's missing a shoe!"

"Excuse me," Nevaeh calls to the woman. "She's the horse that lost a shoe, right? My father is the farrier. Vernon Knowles."

"Yes, this is Zellie," the woman says as she runs her hand

over the horse's back. "She came to us last week with three other horses from the same place. All of them were removed for abuse. Isn't she a beauty? That's right, Zellie, we're talking about you," she sing-songs, "and the nice man is here to put your shoe back on."

The woman's hair is blond and her eyes are blue, and the way she smiles at us reminds me of Mom. Like she's happy just to see you. She holds the rope and the horse tosses her head back and forth like she's saying no the only way she can.

"I'm Nevaeh, and this is my friend Harvard. I'll let my dad know you're coming."

Nevaeh grabs my hand and pulls me in the direction of Mr. Knowles. I hear her words in my head, *my friend Harvard*. It makes it official—I have my first Kettle Hole friend!

Mr. Knowles is unloading his toolbox. Nevaeh puts her hand on her father's arm and tries to stop him.

"Dad, don't shoe that horse," Nevaeh whispers. "There's something wrong with her."

Mr. Knowles pulls the hoof stand out of the back of the truck.

"Honey, it's an easy thirty dollars. She's paying extra because it's last minute."

"Her eyes are wild, and her ears are pinned back. And she bit another horse in the pasture for no reason."

"It's only one shoe. Don't worry. I'll get it on before she knows what happened."

"Remember what you always say? *Never trust a horse. They have brains in them and get ideas just like you and me.*"

139

"That's true, but sometimes you have to trust them some to get a job done," Mr. Knowles answers, tying on his leather apron.

The woman leads Zellie over to Mr. Knowles.

"Thanks for coming on such short notice! My wife is a vet, and she's on an emergency call herself. I'm Ava and this is Zellie. It's her left rear shoe."

"Ava? Spelled A-v-a?" I ask.

"Yes," she says.

"Nevaeh is heaven backwards and I'm Harvard frontwards. You're lucky. You're Ava frontwards and backwards."

"I never thought of it that way. You do have a point," Ava says, holding the rope and standing by Zellie's head.

Mr. Knowles gives Nevaeh the nippers and the rasp to hold for him. She stands off to the side, and she's not smiling. Her eyes are fixed on Zellie.

Mr. Knowles puts a hand on the horse's side. Her body shivers like she's cold.

"Let's take a look at that hoof," Mr. Knowles says.

He bends his knees and starts to pick up her back left leg.

THWACK.

Zellie's rear leg strikes forward at Mr. Knowles. He groans and lowers himself to the ground, holding his shin.

"Dad!" Nevaeh cries out, kneeling down next to him.

"Whaddya know." Mr. Knowles's face, more than his voice, shows the pain he's in. "She's clever with her feet, that mare. She cow-kicked me a good one. Pass that rag, Nevaeh."

Nevaeh gives him a white rag from the toolbox. Mr. Knowles presses it quickly to his shin.

"Oh my, I'm so sorry. I'll put Zellie away and be right back," Ava says, and leads the horse toward the barn. Zellie keeps looking back like she's not done with the fight she started.

When Mr. Knowles lifts the rag, I notice that the gash is deeper and longer than any I've seen before. With Roger as a brother, I've seen my share of injuries. He has scars on his chin, his lip, and two on the same knee.

"Does it hurt a lot?" Nevaeh asks Mr. Knowles.

"Cow-kick? How can a horse cow-kick?" I ask. "And is *cow-kick* one word or two?"

I half thought that might make Nevaeh laugh, but she doesn't answer.

"I'll say it stings, for sure. Nevaeh, pass me that roll of duct tape in the bottom of the toolbox," Mr. Knowles directs her.

She gives him a roll of gray duct tape, and he covers the cut with the rag, then tears off pieces of duct tape and wraps it around the rag. The homemade (home made) bandage looks like something from a war movie.

Ava comes back by herself. I'm pretty sure she put Zellie in horse time-out.

"Are you okay? How can I help?" she asks Mr. Knowles, squatting down to look at his leg.

"I'm fine, but I'd better get on home and tend to this."

He lifts himself up, wincing when his left foot touches the ground.

"Zellie must have had a bad experience with a farrier before. I'll talk to my wife about getting her sedated before we try again. Do you want to clean it up at the house? Can I drive you home?" Ava's blue eyes are watery, like she's about to cry.

"No need of that. We'll manage, won't we, Nevaeh?"

"Yes." Nevaeh drops the rasp and nippers back in the toolbox. They make a loud clanking sound.

Mr. Knowles limps over to the truck.

"Here, please take this for your time." Ava runs after him holding out two twenty-dollar bills.

Mr. Knowles doesn't hesitate. He shakes his head no and holds up his hand.

"You can't pay me for what I didn't do," he says, leaning on the hood of the truck as he makes his way over to the driver's-side door.

Ava seems surprised and looks at the money like she's not sure what to do with it now.

"Help me put the toolbox in the truck," Nevaeh says to me, and we each take a side of the handle the way we did when we carried the bucket full of ant dirt.

Ava offers the money to Nevaeh.

"Please take this for your father's time."

Nevaeh hesitates for a second, then shakes *her* head.

"No need of that," she says, just like Mr. Knowles.

Ava looks very sad. She watches me and Nevaeh lift the toolbox and the hoof stand into the back of the truck. Nevaeh gets in the truck next to Mr. Knowles, and then it's just me and Ava standing there. She holds the money out. I lift *both* my hands in the air.

"Sorry," I say.

Mr. Knowles presses the gas pedal with his right leg and

holds his duct-taped left leg with one hand. When we drive over bumpy roads, he clenches his teeth. Nevaeh keeps looking over at her father's hurt leg. When she breathes out I hear a whistling sound. She doesn't take the little notebook out of the glove compartment. If she did, she'd have to write:

July 10: Second Chances
Horse Haven: No shoe on
Zellie: 0 dollars

"Do you want me to drive us home? I think I could do it," Nevaeh asks Mr. Knowles.

Of all the things I've ever heard Nevaeh say, this one surprises me the most. Mr. Knowles doesn't answer right away, like he's really considering letting his ten-year-old daughter drive the truck.

"Nah, we're almost there," he finally says.

We pass the place where we stopped to see the kettle hole, then drive by Mrs. Sidelinger's yellow house with the weeping willow in the front yard.

"Are we going to the hospital?" I ask Mr. Knowles.

"No, it's gotta be a lot worse than this nick to send me to the emergency room," he says.

I'm pretty sure it's a lot worse than a nick, but I remember all the papers with Earlene Knowles's name on them in the glove compartment.

"When we get back, I'll find my father," I say. "He'll know what to do."

TWENTY-FOUR

Stitches

I rush into the house. Dad is bent over the ant farm again, but turns around when he hears my footsteps. I get right to the point.

"A mean horse named Zellie with pinned-back ears cow-kicked Nevaeh's dad in the shin. The cut is deeper than any of Roger's, and Mr. Knowles won't go to the hospital. I thought since you have your doctor bag here, you could help him."

Dad doesn't ask where I met Zellie or what a cow-kick is or why Mr. Knowles won't go to the hospital. He straightens up even more, then goes into action, the way he used to when the hospital paged him. He disappears into the coat closet and comes out with the brown leather bag with his initials, M.C., on the side. Then he's gone out the front door so fast I have to run to keep up. Before I leave, I take a quick backwards peek at the blackboard. Under **PUPA** there's a bigger banana shape that looks like a cocoon with a black dot on one end.

Mr. Knowles lies on the couch. Nevaeh is untying the laces on his boots and gently pulls the boots off, first one and then the other.

"You're here to get me out of another mess, are you, Marshall?" Mr. Knowles says.

"It works both ways, Vern. First let's see what we're dealing with," Dad says. He sets his bag on the kitchen table and goes over to the sink. He washes his hands and dries them on a paper towel. Then he kneels down next to Mr. Knowles. He doesn't comment about the rag or the gray duct tape.

"Nevaeh, are there scissors handy?" Dad asks her.

She finds them in the table drawer and passes them to him.

Dad looks up at us.

"Harvard, can you and Nevaeh wait at the house in case Roger gets dropped off early from his playdate?"

Nevaeh doesn't move.

"I can stay if you want me to," she says to her father.

"I'll be fine," he answers, closing his eyes as Dad starts snipping into the duct tape. "And you were right about that mare. I should have listened to my horse girl."

Nevaeh stays by her father's side. I've seen Dad stitch up Roger's cuts, so I know if Mr. Knowles needs stitches, Dad will make them so even, you'd think he used a ruler to space them out.

"My dad is very good at this," I say. "And I've got a lot of things to show you at the house."

She slowly follows me, looking back at her father once more before the door closes.

The first thing I show her is what's on the blackboard in the living room.

"Here's Dad's new artwork," I say.

She admires the egg and the larvae and pupae.

"That's really good."

"Check out the ant farm. I think Tenna knows you're here. She's waving her antenna at you."

Nevaeh looks at the ant farm while I work in the kitchen.

"Lunchtime," I announce, putting a plate and a glass in front of her. "Honey sandwiches, apple slices, and sugar water."

"Ant food."

"Exactly, minus the flies," I answer, getting my own plate and cup.

"You think your father can fix my dad up okay?" she asks, taking a sip of the sugar water. I mixed a big spoonful of sugar in each of our water glasses.

"I *know* he can."

"I'm sorry you didn't get to go to Mrs. Sidelinger's today, but I should stay home and help my dad tomorrow."

"That's all right. I know the way there now."

Nevaeh and I start on our honey sandwiches.

"The ant at the end of the smallest tunnel isn't moving very much," she says.

"Yeah, she was in that same spot when I gave them a slice of carrot yesterday, and she didn't come to taste it like the others did. I hope she's just tired and not sick."

"Me too."

I'm trying to come up with something else to distract her when Nevaeh wanders over to the blackboard and picks up the chalk. I wait to see if she's going to write a poem, maybe a horse poem about Zellie, but she starts drawing instead.

Under **ADULT** in Dad's list of **EGG**, **LARVA**, **PUPA**, and **ADULT**, Nevaeh draws a worker ant. She goes back and forth from the ant farm to the blackboard as she works. It's a very detailed picture. She draws the ant head with its long antennae, outlines the diamond-shaped thorax, and makes the stripes on the abdomen. She even draws the way ant legs are thinner at the bottom and how the mandible looks like two curved claws.

Drawing is a good distraction, but I know Nevaeh is still thinking about her father, because she keeps checking the clock on the wall. When Dad comes back she's coloring in the worker ant and drops the chalk on the floor.

"Your father is fine, Nevaeh," he says right away, "but he's going to have to take it easy for a while."

"Thank you, Dr. Corson. I'll make sure he rests up," she says, and is gone out the door before I can say goodbye.

"You were right, Harvard. It *was* a deep laceration, and it needed quite a few stitches," Dad says. Instead of putting his doctor bag back in the closet, he sets it down near the desk. The house ants come out of a crack in the wall I didn't know was there. They circle Dad's bag and two of them climb up and stop right under the initials, like they're trying to figure out what M.C. means. Dad walks right past them.

After dark, I climb out on the roof, lie back, and look at the sky. There are so many stars, and it feels like they're very close. I've never seen stars this close and clear before. I think about calling Mom and telling her that stars really do twinkle. I want to tell her what happened today, but I don't want to get her hopes up that Dad is starting to forgive himself. Working on a cow-kicked leg in a barn house isn't the same as taking care of sick babies in a hospital.

Which reminds me that even though I didn't get to visit Mrs. Sidelinger today, there's still tomorrow to ride my bike to the yellow house with the weeping willow in the front yard.

TWENTY-FIVE

Weeping Willow

In the morning the dish towel is already off the ant farm, and the ant that was resting in the short tunnel isn't in the same spot. The ants aren't carrying anyone to the graveyard or covering new dead ants with dirt, so I guess she's recovered. I do notice one ant partway up the bark, like she wanted to climb to the top but couldn't make it.

The worker ants are busy dusting and feeding Tenna's eggs. I get closer to the farm and notice something I missed yesterday.

"Dad! Some of the eggs look like your larva drawing. They're longer and they have mouths. The workers are feeding them."

Dad pumps his fist as if I just slid into home base and scored a winning run.

"This is a red-letter day for our ant project. To be able to observe the process of metamorphosis firsthand. How many people are privileged to do that?"

"Three?"

I can't imagine what Dad will do when the larvae turn into pupae. Throw them a party?

"What am I doing today?" Roger says as he comes into the kitchen wearing only his pajama bottoms.

"We don't have a playdate set for today. But we could invite a friend over if you want," Dad offers.

"No, I want a playdate with Harvard."

Roger sits on my lap and puts his arms around my neck. He gives me his best little-brother smile. I see the ridged white nubs of grown-up teeth poking out of his gums.

"I was planning to go on a bike ride this morning," I say, "by myself."

"I can ride my bike with you."

"You know if you get tired along the way, you still have to ride all the way back."

Roger hugs me tighter.

"I never get tired."

"I'm going to remember you said that, Roger."

"I'm going to remember it, too, Harvard."

"Where are you riding to?" Dad asks.

I was hoping to avoid this conversation, but I tell as much of the truth as I can.

"When Mr. Knowles drove to the emergency shoeing

call, we passed a yellow house with a giant weeping willow out front. I'm going there."

Dad takes his pen out of his pocket and writes something on his pad.

"You noticed the hemlock trees before. And now this willow. Would you be interested in studying the trees of Maine for another project?"

I can see Dad is ready to buy the biggest book on forests he can find and have us counting tree rings and identifying leaves. I answer with my favorite line from my favorite book.

"Can I get back to you on that?"

And even though I didn't say yes to studying trees, he writes down more things on the pad.

It's downhill almost all the way to the yellow house. People in cars going past us wave, and I wave back. Roger's antennae bob in front of him as he pedals. The sun is hot on my neck and arms.

"I told you I never get tired," Roger informs me, coasting his bike down the biggest hill.

I didn't think ahead to what I'd say when we got to Mrs. Sidelinger's house. I imagined us knocking on the door and her inviting us in for lemonade. I pictured tall glasses with ice in them and lemonade as sweet as sugar water. Maybe her house would have air-conditioning. Somehow when Roger wasn't listening, I'd find a way to tell her about Dad's mistake.

Mrs. Sidelinger isn't home. I knock three times to be sure. Then Roger tap-knocks with his antennae until he notices what's on the side of the house.

"Playground!" Roger throws off his helmet and runs toward a kid's play area with a trampoline and a slide.

"Not a playground. Someone's house," I yell, but he keeps going.

It's even hotter than before, but it's shady under the willow tree. I climb on the lowest curved limb and sit there with the hanging branches all around me.

Roger is jumping on the trampoline and I'm in the weeping willow when a blue minivan pulls in the driveway. A woman with red hair gets out, then slides open the side door. Two little girls are in the back seat. They're almost the same height, and both girls are wearing identical flowered bathing suits.

"I like your playground!" Roger shouts to them, and the girls hold hands and run toward the trampoline.

I hurry over to explain why we're here.

"I'm Harvard Corson and that's my brother, Roger." I continue the way people in Kettle Hole introduce each other, starting with the oldest relative who lived there. "My great-grandfather was Harvard Corson, and *his* daughter was my grandmother Julia Corson. And my father is Marshall Corson. He's renting Vernon Knowles's place for the summer."

The woman looks startled when I say Dad's name.

"I'm Lin Sidelinger," she says, "and those are my girls."

"Are they twins?" I ask.

"Yes, they are."

"I'll get my brother out of your yard. He thinks this is a playground. I tried to tell him it wasn't. We rode our bikes to see you. Or at least I did. Roger just wanted to come with me."

"You came to see me?"

"Yes." I look up at the woman, who's twisting her long hair around her fingers and watching her daughters and Roger. They're all laughing like this is a playdate Dad set up.

"I thought you could talk to my father," I say.

The woman stops playing with her hair and looks straight at me.

"Me?"

When I planned what to say, I didn't think how it would feel to meet a woman who found her little boy dead in his car seat.

"Yes." I swallow hard. "He made a mistake and he can't forgive himself."

The minute the words are out, I forget the rest of what I planned to say. I realize what a big mistake the whole visit is.

Mrs. Sidelinger starts crying.

She covers her mouth with her hand, and tears run down her face.

"I heard about what happened with your dad and the baby," she says, and I think, *Yes, direct from Campbell's mother.*

I didn't mean to make her cry. For once, no words blurt out.

Then, I'm crying, too.

Maybe it's because she has a *weeping* willow on her lawn?

We both stand there in the sun. And I really wish Mom was here, because she'd know what to do.

Mrs. Sidelinger wipes her eyes with her arm and puts a hand on my shoulder. I rub my eyes.

"You're staying at the Knowleses' place?" she asks.

"Yes."

"I will try. I will try and visit your father," she says.

"Thank you" is all I can say, and I call to Roger that we need to leave.

As Roger is waving goodbye to the girls, Mrs. Sidelinger leans toward me and says, very softly, "He may never completely get over it, but he may find a way to move on with his life."

And then I'm left with my brother and the long uphill ride back.

"Why did you make me leave?" Roger whines. "I was having fun at the playground."

"We weren't invited."

"Then why did we go there?"

We're not even halfway up the hill when Roger gets off his bike.

"I can't pedal any more. My legs hurt." He drops the bike and sits in the dirt on the side of the road.

"It's good for your legs. You're building muscle, Roger."

I tense the biceps in my right arm and squeeze it to show him what I mean.

"I don't *want* muscle. I'm tired."

"It's not that far. And I thought you never got tired," I remind him.

"Mommy would carry me."

"Mommy's not here," I say.

Roger bursts into tears. He cries and yells, his face getting redder and redder.

"I'm HOT. And I'm thirsty. You didn't bring drinks like Mommy does. I'm DYING of thirst."

If Mom *was* here, I'd let her deal with Roger's meltdown. I'd ride my bike until I couldn't hear his crying anymore. I might keep riding until I'd been on all twenty-three miles of Kettle Hole roads.

I pick him up and hang him over my shoulder.

"Would Mommy carry you like this?" I joke.

"No!" Roger yells, kicking his legs in my face.

I set him down.

"I can't carry you back, but you can ride with me on my bike. We'll have to leave yours here."

"Okay."

So that's what we do. Roger sits on my bike seat and grabs on to my shirt. I pedal standing up, pumping my legs hard to make it up the rest of the hill. He cries the whole way back.

When we get to the house, Dad is sitting in a chair on the porch looking at his phone. He jumps up when he sees us.

"Why is Roger crying? What happened?" he says.

"Ask Roger," I answer.

Roger stops crying long enough to complain. "It was the worst playdate ever. I'm going to call Mommy and tell her what Harvard did."

"What did you do, Harvard?" Dad gives me a concerned look.

"I didn't do anything. He got tired and thirsty." My voice gets louder. "You're the one who brought a five-year-old six states away from his mother! Isn't it obvious? He misses Mom."

I don't mean to shout, but I'm ready to have my own meltdown.

Dad doesn't get angry or shout back. Instead, he turns away from me, but not before I see that he's crying, too.

I lower my voice. "Roger's bicycle is on the side of the road next to the ditch. And can I borrow your phone to make a call?"

Dad turns around and gives me his phone. He's stopped crying but his eyes are red. He doesn't ask who I want to call.

No one sees me when I climb the arbor onto the roof.

I try FaceTime and when Mom answers I see her for the first time since we came to Kettle Hole. She's wearing a blue shirt instead of a white lab coat. It looks like she's in a restaurant with giant stuffed fish and nets on the wall behind her.

"Harvard!" Mom waves at me. "You called during the day instead of at night. How are you doing? I can't tell where you are. Are you in the house or outside?"

"I'm *on* the house. Where are you? You're not at work."

"Did you say *on the house*? I'm on a mini vacation. Reena was going to the beach for a few days and convinced me to come with her. She knows it's been a hard few months for everyone."

Mom turns the phone so I can see Reena, who is sitting across from her. Mom's friend gives me a big smile and a double thumbs-up. Her skin is brown, and her black hair is almost the same color as Mom's, but curlier.

"You're on vacation?" I ask Mom, when she turns the phone back.

"Yes, let me see if I can go out on the deck and show you the beach. It's so pretty."

"I don't care about the *beach*," I say. "I was calling to tell you Roger's been crying for you and Dad is crying, too. In case you wanted to know. I didn't know you were on *va-ca-tion*."

I pronounce each syllable in *va-ca-tion*.

Mom's smile disappears.

"Of course I want to know, Harvard," she says, and then it happens. I didn't mean to do it, but now I've made every single person I've talked to today cry, including myself.

Mom pats her face with a napkin. "Don't hang up, Harvard. I'm okay. What is it you want? What do you need me to do?"

Before I respond, I think of all the things I want.

I want Mrs. Sidelinger to tell Dad how she can still live in the place where she made the biggest mistake. I want Dad to forgive himself. I want the worker ants to stop getting sick and dying. I want Roger to be able to hold Mom's hand before he falls asleep. I want Nevaeh to get Joker back in the fall. I want her to find a friend who can read her mind, to keep her mother's promise.

I want Mom to see the dark that is so dark and hear the spooky sound of coyotes howling in the night. And show her the droopy hemlock branches, the weeping willow that hangs to the ground, and the shaggy bark on the sugar maple trees near the barn house.

Mom watches me, waiting for my answer.

"I want you to come to Kettle Hole," I say.

"When?"

"How soon can you get here?"

Mom's eyes dart over to Reena, then back to me.

Then she tells one of our old but good parasite jokes.

"You know it's not easy to find a new host."

I smile at Mom and she smiles back.

"I'll change my ticket to Old Home Day and take the time off earlier. I can be there in three days. Tell Dad I'll talk to him tonight," she says.

"Great!" I say. And I realize I called because I was mad, and I called because Roger cried for her, but now that I know Mom is really coming, three days can't go by fast enough.

TWENTY-SIX

A in Ants

"Guess what? I asked Mom to come, and she'll be here in three days! She said she's gonna call you later," I tell Dad.

"That's wonderful," Dad says, and takes his pad out of his pocket. "I'll have to shop for a special first-night supper."

"I can show her the snow!" Roger bounces on the couch, all happy now. That's one great thing about my brother—he never stays mad for long.

The house ants stop and do their front leg clapping.

I study the ant farm while Dad answers Roger's questions. More of Tenna's eggs have turned into larvae, and they're squirming around and being fed by the workers.

"How's Mr. Knowles?" I ask Dad.

"I checked on him today while you and Roger were out," Dad says. "I redressed the bandage and it's looking good. No signs of infection."

At Roger's bedtime, I listen from my room as Dad tells the bedtime story.

"When I turned five, it was a bitterly cold January and my grandfather took me ice fishing with him for the first time. He said if I caught a fish, we'd cook it for supper. I'd never walked on a frozen lake before. As we made our way across, the ice made loud cracking and booming sounds and they scared me."

"They wouldn't scare *me*," Roger says.

"That's good. It's nothing to be scared of. Anyway, so my grandfather pulled the hand auger, the tip-ups, the sieve, and the bait on a sled. We walked until the shoreline seemed miles away. I was dressed warmly, but my face got cold, especially my nose, so I held my wool mittens over my face while my grandfather twisted the auger into the ice to make the holes. He used the sieve to scoop the slush and ice chunks out from the holes before he set up the tip-ups."

Then it's quiet except for Roger's snoring.

I go across the hall and stand in the doorway of Roger's room.

"What's up, Harvard?" Dad whispers.

"When are you going to *finish* the story? What *happened* out there on the lake? Did you catch a fish or *not*?"

I shake my arms out in front of me with each question. And my voice gets louder and louder.

"No, we *didn't* catch any fish that day."

"What kind of a fishing story is that?"

"Not every fishing story ends with a fish," Dad says.

I look up at the cracks in Roger's ceiling. They're shaped like mushrooms.

"Do you have a different story you can tell next time?" I ask politely. I don't want to make him cry again.

"As a matter of fact, I do," he says, and gazes ahead like he's already thinking of the new story.

I hope Dad tells the story of when he and Vern went to the kettle hole pond. I want to know if Mr. Knowles swam underwater and what it was like for Dad to pull him out with a rope.

Sometime during the night I wake from the best dream ever. I was dreaming that my feet were touching the bottom of the kettle hole pond, and it wasn't mucky or sandy. It was as hard and solid as the granite step to the front porch. I was walking on the bottom, but my head was still out of the water, so I could see all around me. The sun was shining, and the sky was blue.

Instead of being in the water, I'm in my bed. There's a light on in the hallway, and I hear noises downstairs. I start down the stairs but stop on step five.

Dad is bending over the ant farm with long tweezers in his hand. The cover is off, and he reaches in and takes something out. Something he puts in his hand and carefully examines before wrapping it in a tissue and disappearing into the kitchen. I hear the garbage can lid open and close.

I start down the stairs and forget about skipping creaky step two.

Dad is back next to the ant farm and spins around at the sound. "What are you doing up? Trouble sleeping?" He closes his hand around the tweezers.

I look in the ant farm. The sick ant that was halfway up the bark is gone.

"I saw what you just did. You threw out a dead ant," I say quietly. I don't even feel like shouting.

Dad sets the tweezers on the windowsill and puts the cover back on the ant farm. He sits down at the table.

"I thought you'd be upset about the ants falling ill. It was our summer project," Dad says.

I sit across from him.

"You could have told me what you were doing. I knew some of them were sick. Nevaeh and I hid the first dead ants in the ant graveyard so YOU wouldn't know they died. And do you know *why* the ants are big and black instead of small and red like western harvester ants are supposed to be? Because the western harvester ants you ordered were dead when they came. So Nevaeh and I found other ants and put them in the tube instead."

Dad stares at me, looking stunned, then studies the ant farm.

"Well, I'll be," he says, shaking his head.

"Our summer project is great," I say. "Look at Tenna. Do you think anyone else has a queen ant and fourteen eggs and larvae?"

"I guess you're right about that." He shakes his head again. "So you found other ants?"

"Yes. Right here in the house. Nevaeh helped me catch them. *Camponotus pennsylvanicus.* That's Latin for carpenter ants."

Dad leans toward me, a big smile on his face.

"My grandfather would have been proud of you. He always said, *Use what's at hand.* Of course, he probably never expected it would apply to finding ants, but that's what you did. You used what was around you."

"Does that mean I get an A in ants?"

Dad sits back in his chair and laughs. I don't know if he's laughing at what I said or the idea of my great-grandfather Harvard seeing an ant farm full of carpenter ants. All I know is how good it feels to hear that sound again.

TWENTY-SEVEN

Red Roses

Roger has big plans for Mom's visit. He talks about them constantly. Besides showing her the hail, he wants her to meet his new playdate friends. Dad is as busy as the ants, cooking and cleaning the house for Mom's visit. When he's done inside, he washes the outside of the windows. I clean my room and put away the dishes.

"Roger and I are off to the dump," he says, loading the trunk of the car with garbage bags.

"If we were ants, we'd have a garbage dump in a corner of the house," I point out.

He hands me the broom.

"Here. Please give the porch a good sweeping while we're gone."

While I sweep I look toward the barn and the shaggy maple trees. I want to visit Nevaeh, but then she'd ask about my trip to the yellow house with the weeping willow.

If I knew it was going to be a mistake to talk to Mrs. Sidelinger, I wouldn't have gone there. But I only figured it out afterward.

I thought I was protecting Dad by not telling him about the dead ants, and he thought he was protecting me by doing the same thing. Both of us were wrong.

I'm starting to worry if asking Mom to come was also a mistake. She might not care how the air in Kettle Hole smells like grass and pine cones (pinecones) or that Dad's doctor bag is in the living room. She could get here, look around, and wish she was back home.

My original plan—to wait until Tenna's eggs hatched for Mom to come—seemed perfect when I first came up with it. I thought seeing the new ants hatch would make Dad so happy he'd be like he was before the mistake. Now I'm not so sure.

Was it fair to catch ants and put them in the ant farm just because Dad was excited about the project? Even though they have dirt from the woods and moss and bark and a pebble, they're separated from the house ants and stuck between two pieces of glass. Do they like the honey and apples, or would they rather find crickets and seeds in the grass?

What if my Old Home Day poem raffle idea is a mistake, too? Suppose no one guesses Nevaeh's word and all she has is a fishbowl of wrong answers and no friend who can read her mind?

Did McKenzie get my letter, read it, and tear it up?

There should be an alarm that goes off when you're about to make a mistake. BEEP BEEP BEEP. Then you can stop what you're doing before you get it wrong. BEEP. Wrong idea. Think again. BEEP. This horse is going to kick you. BEEP. Close your mouth before you make someone cry.

I'm so busy sweeping and thinking I don't hear Nevaeh until she's right next to me, holding red roses in a glass jar.

"I cut these for your mom from my mother's garden. Dad said she's coming soon, right?"

"Yes, she's flying into Bangor the day after tomorrow and renting a car. Do you want to put the roses inside?"

"Sure," she says, and we go into the house. "How about in the middle of the table?" she asks.

"Okay," I agree.

"How long is she staying?" she asks, placing the vase in the exact center of the table. She carefully arranges the four roses so whichever way you look at it, you see a whole rose.

"I don't know."

"Well, keep checking the water in the jar before she gets here."

"I will. How's your father's leg?"

"Better. Your dad says it's healing good."

This is when I need to hear the BEEP BEEP.

"If you don't want to do the poem raffle, we don't have to," I say.

Nevaeh is stroking a rose and pulls her fingers away like the petals are hot.

"It was *your* idea. Now you don't want to do it?"

166

"I do, but what if no one can read your mind? If all the guesses are wrong? What if your mom made a mistake with the read-your-mind promise?"

"A mistake?"

The BEEP BEEP warning, if I had one, would have to be very loud now, because once I start talking I don't stop.

"Yeah, what if she meant find a friend who *can* read your mind but doesn't, because who wants someone knowing what they're thinking all the time. Or she meant: Find a friend. Period. Who can read your mind? Question mark. Two different sentences. Like she's wondering who can read anyone's mind."

"You weren't there," Nevaeh says.

"And what about the promise to your father? Not to take state aid for the hospital bills and pay them all himself. What if she was wrong about that? That she didn't think how it could be a problem if your father got hurt but wouldn't go to the hospital because he didn't have the money?"

"You think I don't understand my own mother's promises? Or that her promise to Dad was a mistake? And now you don't want to do the raffle? After we made the posters and everything?"

"That's not what I'm saying."

"It sounds like it *is* what you're saying," Nevaeh answers.

She stares at me and I can tell she's trying to decide how mad she is. If she's mad enough to walk out and slam the door.

"Dad knew about the dying ants all along," I say. "I caught him getting rid of a dead ant the other night. And I told him about the *camponotus pennsylvanicus*. That they weren't western harvester ants."

"What did he say?"

"He laughed. He thought it was very funny."

"I guess it kinda is."

Nevaeh smiles a little, and I'm glad I didn't lose my first Kettle Hole friend.

"I'm the one who made the biggest mistake." I point a finger at myself. "I made Mrs. Sidelinger cry."

"Oh no. I forgot to ask if you went there yesterday."

"Oh yes. And you know what she told me? She said Dad may never completely get over it. What if she comes here and tells him that? It'll only make things worse."

"Oh no," Nevaeh says again, and flops down on the couch.

There's one more thing I'm itching to say. That the no-smoking promise is backwards, like Nevaeh's name, a promise that should have been her mother's to keep, not hers.

But I don't. Instead, I drop down on the couch next to her.

"Yrros," I say. "I really do want to do the raffle."

TWENTY-EIGHT

Mom

Since the night I caught Dad throwing the dead ant in the trash, there aren't any more dish towel–covered ant farm secrets, and just as mysteriously as it started, the ants stop getting sick. No more slow-moving ants rest in the tunnels. The beginning of a brand-new tunnel appears. There are more eyeless hungry-mouthed larvae, constantly being fed by the worker ants as they grow bigger and bigger. Two of the larvae turn into pupae, spinning silk cocoons that look like Dad's drawing. Sometimes it takes me a minute to find Tenna in the pile of squirmy larvae and hurrying-around workers.

We're outside when Mom gets here. The front lawn grass is as short as Dad's new Bob's Barber Shop haircut.

Sheets and pillowcases hang on the clothesline. Dad plays catch with Roger.

Mom gets out of the car and kneels down as Roger runs straight into her arms. Her dress is purple, and her earrings are little gold hoops. Her curly black hair is loose. Mom says she should have had braces when she was little, but I like the way her teeth look when she smiles.

Roger is in full tattletale mode.

"Dad tells the same boring bedtime story every night, and once I saw Harvard up on the roof. And Gordon's grandmother got mad when we dug in her garden. We wanted to see what it was like to live in a tunnel like the ants, and she called us little voles."

"Oh my." Mom looks over Roger's head at Dad.

"Dee . . ." Dad walks across the lawn toward Mom.

They wrap their arms around each other, Roger still stuck to Mom's side the way ant eggs stick to each other.

"Marshall, this place is good for you. I can see that."

"I've missed you terribly," Dad says.

"Harvard, my boy," Mom calls to me. I'm sitting on the granite porch step that's cool even in the heat.

I lift a hand in the air. Suddenly I'm so tired. We've only been in Kettle Hole for five weeks, but it feels like I've been looking after Roger and trying to cheer Dad up since forever. Plus trying to keep an entire ant farm alive.

"Mommy, come see your surprise." Roger pulls on Mom's dress. "It's in the house and you won't believe what it is."

I follow them in. Roger leads Mom to the freezer and puts a pile of hailstones in her hand.

"It's snow," he explains.

"Wow! Snow in July. It's so cold. Roger, that's the best surprise. I never would have guessed it in a million years. Thank you!"

I think Mom's overdoing the shocked act, but Roger is buying it.

"Here." I hold up the vase of roses to show Mom. "My friend Nevaeh cut these for you."

Mom leans over and sniffs. "Intoxicating!"

"And this must be the ant farm," she says. "Dad said you worked on building it together. What's happening in there?"

"That's Tenna." I point to her. She's surrounded by her workers. "She's the biggest one, the queen. And those are her eggs, and larvae and pupae. All the other ants are workers."

"Are the workers licking Tenna? It looks like some kind of grooming behavior is going on," Mom observes. "I'm curious why they do that. I've read that some insect saliva has antibiotic and antifungal properties."

"ANT-ibiotic and ANT-ifungal! Good ant jokes, Mom."

Then I find *The Natural Genius of Ants* and hold it up so Mom can see the big ant on the cover.

"The answer is probably in here. But yes, they also lick the eggs and the larvae. Tenna does it, too. They even lick each other."

The minute the words are out of my mouth, I realize what I said and who is listening. Dad raises his eyebrows.

"Licking?" Roger puts his face up to the side of the ant farm. "You're right. They *are* licking each other."

At supper, all four of us sit together at the table. I can

smell the vegetable soup in our bowls, the rolls Dad made, and the scent of the roses in the middle of the table. Mom strokes a rose petal the way Nevaeh did, then lifts up the vase to smell them again.

"That was very thoughtful of her to bring me roses. Tell me about your friend, Nevaeh," she says.

"She made the snow and—" Roger starts to say.

Mom interrupts him. "I was asking Harvard, Roger. You can get a turn after."

"Nevaeh lives in the barn house next door, and she has a ladder going up to her loft room," I say. "And she keeps track of how much money her father makes when he goes shoeing. In a special notebook. She writes poems, too, short ones, mostly on envelopes she keeps in her pocket."

"Does she?" Mom says.

While I'm speaking Roger picks the carrots out of his soup and piles them up on his napkin.

The more I talk about Nevaeh, the more things I think of.

"She knows places in the woods to collect moss, and she can tell if a horse has something wrong with it. But she's not afraid of horses. She'll go right up to them, even a big horse. And she doesn't smoke," I add at the end, in case we visit when Nevaeh has a cigarette lit.

"Glad to hear that," Mom says.

"And Nevaeh grew up in Kettle Hole," I continue. "Did you know this isn't my first trip to Kettle Hole? The man at the post office said he met me when Dad came for his grandfather's funeral."

"That's true. I was away visiting my father in the DR

when Dad's grandfather died, and he took you with him," Mom says.

"Eels in the Gulf of Maine swim all the way to the Sargasso Sea, where they first hatched as larvae," Dad comments, like we're continuing the conversation we had a week ago about animals who find their way back to their birthplace. "It's an incredible journey, if you consider they make a return trip of fifteen hundred miles after almost thirty years."

"I wonder what the larvae look like, if they look anything like ant larvae." I blow on my soup spoon before taking a sip.

Then I think of something that hadn't occurred to me before.

"When you brought me to Kettle Hole for the funeral, did you take me in the kettle hole pond?"

Dad looks horrified.

"You were only a year old, and it was November. Why would I do that?"

"Mr. Knowles says there's a story that people who go in the waters of the kettle hole pond always return here. Maybe if you'd gone in the water with Mr. Knowles when you were a boy, or taken me in the water, we'd have come back here before now, like the eels—"

Roger interrupts. "Harvard is doing all the talking. When is my turn?"

"You can have your turn now," Mom says. "What would you like to say?"

"How long will it take you and me to get home on the plane?" Roger asks Mom. He's pulled his chair up close to hers and leans against her when he asks the question.

This is news to me. Mom and Dad look at each other like it's news to them, too.

"You want to go back with Mom?" I ask him. "You don't want to stay and see the larvae hatch and go to Old Home Day?"

Roger takes a roll and dips it in his soup.

"Nope. I want to go home with Mommy," he says. "And see Abuela and Tio Emilio."

"What about Gordon and Iris?" I ask.

"They can come visit me," he says, and hooks his arm around Mom's neck.

"It's up to you, Dee," Dad says.

"We're paying to keep his place in day care. And my mother can help out. I'll see if there's an open seat on the plane," Mom says.

"Get a seat for Harvard, too. Dad can drive the car home," Roger says, like he's now in charge of all the travel plans.

"I promised to help Nevaeh with her table on Old Home Day," I explain.

"Okay. You can stay for that," he says. "And come home after."

When I wake during the night, I follow Roger's snores to Dad's room. He's asleep between Mom and Dad, his hand in Mom's. Dad has an arm across Mom. I stand quietly watching them, and Mom's eyes pop open.

She edges closer to Roger and makes room for me in the bed.

"I missed you," she whispers.

"How long are you staying?" I ask.

"Two more full days," she says. "Then we'll leave the following morning."

Mom's hair is loose on the pillow next to me and its smell reminds me of backhome—the food smells outside the apartment building, the elevator, my room. I lie there with my eyes closed and imagine this is what it feels like to be an ant in a tunnel, with your whole family always an antenna's length away.

TWENTY-NINE

Solving for X

The first of Mom's *two more full days* we go into town. Mom gets a book about earthworms at Kettle Hole Books. She wants to see the house Dad grew up in, so he drives just beyond Cone Heaven and makes a right down a long, straight road.

We go past a brick building with a sign that says KETTLE HOLE MIDDLE SCHOOL, then Dad turns onto a dirt road and stops in front of a small white house surrounded by fields.

"Is there a playground in the back?" Roger asks.

Dad doesn't answer. "It looks like whoever lives there is keeping it up. They put on a new roof. And the fields are mowed."

Mom takes Dad's hand. "I'm so glad I got to see this."

Gordon's grandmother doesn't stay mad about Roger and Gordon tunneling in her garden because she throws a goodbye pool party playdate for Roger on Mom's last full day. She also invites Iris and Dad. That gives me a whole afternoon by myself with Mom.

I didn't write a list like Dad would have, but I've been keeping track of the things I want to show her. Dad's bag. The barn house. Nevaeh and Mr. Knowles. The hemlock grove.

First I point out Dad's doctor bag on the floor in the living room and describe what happened to Mr. Knowles and how Dad knew what to do to fix his leg.

"Your father is an excellent doctor," she says. "The other day I ran into one of the nurses he worked with, and she said they had a set of quadruplets and everyone was wishing Dad was there."

"He can go back if he wants to? What about the mistake?"

I wasn't sure if Dad didn't go back to his work because he couldn't forgive himself or because he wasn't allowed to.

"He can go back anytime. Your father is not the first doctor to make a mistake."

Then we go outside, and Mom takes a deep breath.

"The air doesn't just smell good here, it tastes good, too," she says.

I know what she means. When you sniff really hard, the smell goes into the back of your throat.

I take Mom to the hemlock grove, along the trails Nevaeh

showed me. Mom looks up at the trees and down at the cone-covered ground. I show her where we got the dirt and bark for the ant farm. It's true what Dad said, that the tops of the hemlocks all point in the same direction, which must be east.

"It's so peaceful here," she says. "If I lie down under these majestic trees, I might never want to get up."

After the hemlock grove, we go to the barn house. Nevaeh answers the door.

"Thank you for the lovely roses," Mom says.

Mr. Knowles pulls up his pant leg and shows her the stitches Dad sewed. Mom says she's sorry to hear about Earlene, and Mr. Knowles goes out to the truck and comes back with a stack of papers.

"You're a doctor, right? What do you make of these bills?" he asks. "I told Marshall I don't know how regular folks are supposed to pay for what hospitals cost."

Mom says she doesn't work with people, but that doesn't seem to matter to Mr. Knowles. She looks carefully at each one and agrees with how expensive they are.

"I heard Kettle Hole has a good clinic. Did Earlene ever go there?" Mom says.

"No, she had to get all her care at the cancer center. That's where they charge the big money. Wait till you see this one." Mr. Knowles sorts through the papers. "Yes, here it is. Guess what it cost for a back pillow, no different than what you could buy in town?"

"I have no idea," Mom says.

Mr. Knowles hands her the bill, then looks for another one for her to guess the price.

"This is a lot for you, isn't it, trying to pay off these bills?" Mom looks at the paper.

"I made Earlene a promise. You didn't know her father, but he was just the same. Didn't believe in government programs or charity. He wouldn't even take general assistance from the town when he had his chainsaw accident."

"I see," Mom says.

"Take this one here . . ." Mr. Knowles holds up a bill between two fingers. "What do you think it costs to stay in a hospital room for two nights, nothing else?"

"I couldn't begin to guess," Mom says.

I can tell this is a game that might go on for a long time.

"Mom, did you see the raffle poster Nevaeh made?" I say.

"Ooh, that's lovely." Mom admires the goldfish drawing that's tacked to the wall over the table.

Nevaeh opens the table drawer and takes out drawings I never saw before—the cupola on the barn, red roses in a glass jar, tall shaggy-barked trees. She gives Mom the one of the roses.

We go back to the house with all the things on my mental list done. Check. Check. Check. Check.

Mom hands me a paper bag.

"I got it for you at an interstate rest stop on the drive from the airport to Kettle Hole. They had a gift shop."

It's a book titled *Woods and Trees of Maine*, and there's a pine tree on the cover.

"Thanks," I say. "Did you get anything for Roger?"

"I got him a weather radio, but in my rush to pack, I left it at home."

Mom stands in front of the blackboard and picks up a piece of chalk. She twirls the chalk back and forth between her fingers. There's something about a blackboard that makes you want to write on it. Seeing the ant drawings makes me remember something else.

"Did Dad tell you what happened with the dead ants?"

Mom smiles. "Yes, I heard that was quite the mix-up, wasn't it?"

"When he found out, Dad *laughed*," I tell her. "He laughed just like before. Don't you think Dad is doing better now? He's happy about the ant farm and he took care of Mr. Knowles's leg."

Mom lays down the chalk and turns around. She puts her hands on my shoulders and stares into my eyeballs.

"Harvard, it's not your job to fix everything. You *can't* fix everything, even if you wanted to."

I stare back.

"I heard you talking to Dad at home. You said his guilt was crushing you."

Mom blinks.

"That doesn't mean I don't love him. I adore your father. These past months, I tried very hard to make everything better, but I couldn't. Sometimes you have to wait for the other person to figure things out. And I hate waiting."

"I hate waiting, too."

"I know. Dad is figuring things out for himself. Say you have the equation X plus Y equals Z. You know you want five as your answer, your Z. The challenge is finding what combination of X and Y will get you there. Sometimes I use that principle in my research. I know where I want to end up, Z, and I've got my Y. All I need is to solve for X."

Mrs. Sidelinger said, *He may never completely get over it, but he may find a way to move on with his life.*

"Kettle Hole is Y," I say.

"Smart boy! I remember when you were a little older than Roger is now and Roger was learning how to walk. It was a learning curve and sometimes he'd take two steps and fall. You'd run ahead and put the couch pillows on the floor, so he'd have a soft place to land. Which was very sweet of you. But you know what, you could never predict where he'd fall or if he wouldn't fall at all and would make it all the way across the room by himself."

Mom puts her hand on my cheek. "I guess what I'm say-ing, Harvard, is try to enjoy the rest of the summer and don't worry about Dad. That's not your job."

"Right, I'm too young to have a job, anyway. Don't I have to be fourteen for a work permit?"

Mom laughs.

"Somehow you always make me laugh," she says.

"That's my job. And good luck with your parasite math," I say, making her laugh again.

The next morning, when it's time for Mom and Roger to leave, Roger hugs me tight before he gets in the car.

"I won't go in your room and play with your things," he

says, which is definitely Roger for *I'll be going in your room and playing with your things while you're gone.* "And guess what, I have a window seat on the plane."

"Very cool," I say, and when I hug him back, he licks the side of my face.

Mom wraps her arms around me, and I breathe in her mom smell the way Nevaeh did with her mother's last cigarette.

"No worries. Enjoy," she whispers in my ear.

"You too," I answer.

Mom and Dad hug and kiss for longer than several ant naps' worth.

Then the car backs out of the driveway, and it's just me and Dad left standing there.

"How long are *we* going to be here?" I ask.

Dad says the same thing I said to Roger at supper the first night Mom was here.

"Don't you want to stay and see the ants hatch and go to Old Home Day?"

"I do," I say.

"Me too," he says.

We both watch the empty road.

It's not my job to fix everything, Mom said. Trying to fix things didn't work out the way I planned, anyway. So for now I'll wait and see what happens all by itself.

As we head toward the house, the wind starts blowing. At first, it's a breeze ruffling the tops of the trees, then it becomes something else.

THIRTY

Bomb Cyclone

Over the next few hours, the wind picks up and it starts to rain. The wind blows the rain sideways, and Dad goes in the house to close the windows. Outside on the porch it feels like I'm on the edge of a hurricane, and I don't want to miss it when it comes. Even if it blows me away.

"Harvard, you're going to get very wet," Dad says from the front door.

"I know," I answer. "I like it out here."

He pauses a second.

"All right."

Dad isn't my job anymore. Roger has Mom's hand. The ants stopped dying. All I have to take care of is me. I want to feel the wind that's gusting so hard the house rattles like it might break into pieces. The trees bend lower than I knew trees could bend. A harsh and high-pitched howling starts, but the air smells sweet and flowery, like it blew here from a tropical place.

Dad watches me from a window.

"I'm okay," I mouth, and he moves away. I sit on a porch chair, but I could be on a boat in the sea out in a storm. It's raining so hard I can't see very far into the woods, and the sky is dark, like it's suddenly nighttime.

There's a whishing sound and a sharp crack.

Dad is back at the door with a pot in each hand. He sets them on the ground where the water runs off the edge of the porch roof.

"The power's out so there's no water in the house. Might as well collect what we can off the roof while it's raining, to use for washing dishes and flushing the toilet."

"Did you hear the cracking sound?"

"I did. Lightning could have hit a wire. When it lets up we can check on Vern and Nevaeh. Their power is probably out, too."

"I'll help get more pots," I offer.

Dad and I get everything from baking bowls to a plastic bucket we find in the shed and watch them fill up in a few minutes. There are more cracking sounds and booms. Sheets of water stream down off the roof.

"Stay out with me, Dad. It's amazing!"

I'm surprised when Dad comes and sits on a porch chair. The blowing rain wets his pants and shoes, but he stays.

I don't know how long we sit there, the two of us, while

the wind screeches and the pots and bowls overflow onto the ground. We can't talk over the noise the wind and the rain make. When Dad's cell phone rings, he reaches for it in his back pocket and looks at the screen.

"It's Mom," he says, and goes in the house, standing near the door to get better reception.

The howling doesn't let up. If anything, it's louder and there's a tearing noise like the Velcro on Roger's sneaker straps is being pulled apart, but way louder. First there's the Velcro sound, then more sharp cracks and big thuds, over and over. They sound very close.

"Harvard! Come in the house." The tone of Dad's voice stops me from asking why.

I'm getting up when I hear the loudest crack and thud.

"Yikes!" I scream and run inside, closing the door tight behind me.

"Wow! That was very close," Dad says. "Mom said this storm is hitting the whole East Coast. There are power outages all over because of downed trees. They're calling it a bomb cyclone."

"Bomb cyclone?"

"Two words."

"No, I mean what *is* a bomb cyclone?"

"A very low-pressure system. Hurricane-force winds are blowing from the southeast rather than the northwest. Trees around here are used to having strong winds blow from the northwest, not the southeast, and their root systems aren't prepared for winds coming from an unexpected direction."

"Why did Mom call? Are they back home yet?"

"They made it home, but their flight was very turbulent. Mom said Roger was the only passenger on board having a good time. He informed everyone on the plane that his friend Nevaeh was doing the wind for him."

"Ha!" I laugh, picturing how excited Roger would be to finally get his wind. "Luckily it's hard to fall out of a seat on a plane. I can't wait to tell Nevaeh. When can I go see her?"

Before Dad can answer there's another loud crack and a boom.

"Not until the storm is over," he says.

"Do you think any of the trees will hit the house?"

"I don't think any of them are in striking distance."

"What about the barn house?"

"I don't know."

"Which direction is southeast?" I ask, and Dad points toward the back lawn.

Even though it's only afternoon, it's dim inside. I flip on the overhead light, but nothing happens, and I remember the power is out.

Dad holds his phone up.

"My charge is not going to last long. Neither will the ice cream in the freezer, so help yourself."

There's a tub of vanilla and a tub of Maine blueberry, both from Cone Heaven.

"Good thing Mom came when she did," I tell Dad, helping myself to a bowl of vanilla. "Roger would have been pretty upset if the hail melted before he had a chance to show it to her."

"Very true," Dad says.

I sit in front of the window eating my bowl of ice cream and watch as the wind slowly dies down. The rain stops, but the air still smells like the ocean.

Dad and I are both thinking the same thing, because when the sky brightens he says, "Let's go see how our friends are doing."

THIRTY-ONE

Windfirm

Trees are on the ground everywhere near the barn house, but none landed on the barn. Their snowmen branches are broken off in pieces. Mr. Knowles and Nevaeh are standing next to a fallen sugar maple. Sticking out from under its huge trunk is something red and metal. Something that used to be a truck.

"Your tires are flat," I observe.

Neveah snorts.

"Harvard!" Dad shakes his head at me.

"Oh, we could all use a little humor about now," Mr. Knowles says. "You should have heard the sound it made getting crushed. Sounded like a fox screaming."

"They're down but you didn't cut 'em, so your father can't be mad," I say. "How many fell?"

"We counted fifteen."

"Wow!"

I remember what I wanted to tell Nevaeh.

"Mom and Roger's flight home was very bumpy, and Roger told everyone that you made the wind for him. Mom said he was the only person on the plane who was excited about it."

"You tell Roger I'm taking a break from doing the weather. I don't want him asking for a sandstorm or a blizzard next."

There's something white sticking out of Nevaeh's back pocket.

"Did you write another poem?" I ask, and she hands me the folded envelope.

Storm

You whistled for me
but I didn't come out.
So you banged at the door
and started to shout.

Mom said I'm stronger
than I know.
Do you feel the same way
when your winds blow?

"Yes! That's what I thought when I watched the storm. Like, okay, bring all the rain, take the power, knock the trees down, what are you going to do next?"

"It was scary, though," Nevaeh says.

"Yeah. The trees were loud when they crashed." I rub the rough bark on the maple that crushed Mr. Knowles's truck and look around. I notice something strange.

"Hey, all the trees fell in the same direction. What direction is that?" I point where the tops all fell.

"Northwest," Mr. Knowles says.

"Dee said they're calling the storm a bomb cyclone," Dad says, "with winds blowing in from the southeast."

"That makes sense," Mr. Knowles says. "Trees around here are only windfirm in one direction."

Nevaeh gives me a look, like she's waiting for me to ask if *windfirm* is one word or two, but I just shrug. Someday someone is going to make a rule for which words are one word or two and I'm gonna wait for that. Or make up the rule myself.

"Take my car anytime you need to," Dad says to Mr. Knowles. "The keys are always in it."

Mr. Knowles puts his arm across Dad's shoulders.

"Thanks, my friend. The keys are in my truck, too," Mr. Knowles says, and he and Dad start laughing so hard they bend over with tears streaming down their faces. And every time one of them points to the flattened truck they laugh even harder until they can barely speak.

Nevaeh rolls her eyes at her father. I watch Dad. It only

took a bomb cyclone, fifteen downed trees, and a crushed red pickup to make him laugh until he cried.

"This is our chance," I whisper to Nevaeh. "Now that the trees are on the ground, let's go see if there's treasure hidden in them."

THIRTY-TWO

Acer Saccharum

"Tell me again what your grandfather said about the trees," I ask Nevaeh.

We climb onto the trunks and walk the length of the trees. We stick our hands into holes Nevaeh said were places where owls nested. I really thought there'd be a secret door Nevaeh's grandfather carved into the trees and filled with coins. Or a metal box chained to a high-up branch with a treasure map inside. But there's nothing like that.

It's a funny feeling, balancing on the trunks, because if the trees were still standing, we'd be a hundred feet in the air when we got to the top.

"He said not to tap them or cut them for firewood, that they might have more value in them than the sugar," she says.

"What will happen to them now?" I ask.

"Dad will probably use them for firewood since they're already down. My grandfather only said don't cut them, he didn't say what to do if they fell. Maybe he said that because he liked looking at them and didn't want them cut."

Nevaeh and I sit near the top of a tree. She rests back on a branch and her face is partly covered by leaves. She coughs and coughs, then blows her breath out in a big sigh.

"Do you need to use your inhaler?" I ask, running my fingers over the little bumps and dents in the rough bark.

"I left the red inhaler and the last cigarette in my backpack in the truck. We just got home from a shoeing job when the storm started, and Dad said to run to the house while he unloaded the tools."

"Wow, it's good you got to the house before the trees fell."

I think about what Mr. Knowles said, how it sounded like foxes screaming when the tree hit the truck.

"Yeah," she says, and we're both quiet for a while. "I like your mom," she says. "It was nice of her to look at all those bills with Dad. It's annoying how he's always showing them to people."

"She liked you and your father, too. I bet she frames your rose drawing."

"Look!" Nevaeh moves a branch to the side. "A blue minivan just pulled into your driveway."

"Oh no. Mrs. Sidelinger has a blue minivan," I say, and lower myself onto the ground.

I run through the woods, making detours around the fallen trees, but I'm too late. By the time I'm on the path to the house, Mrs. Sidelinger and Dad are already sitting on the porch chairs talking. I hide behind some of the trees left standing, the ones the storm missed.

I'm not close enough to hear what they're saying, but Mrs. Sidelinger is talking, and Dad is listening. At one point, he lowers his head. Then Dad starts talking, his head still bent down. Mrs. Sidelinger pulls her chair closer to his and leans toward him, her head almost touching his. Dad talks for a long time.

I poke my fingers into the ridges in the bark of the trees. Dad keeps on talking. If he's telling Mrs. Sidelinger about what happened to baby Hope, how much is there to say about it? I made a mistake. I didn't mean to. She died.

My legs are getting crampy from crouching down when Mrs. Sidelinger stands up and Dad walks with her to her car. Before she gets in, they hug. I don't know if Mrs. Sidelinger reaches for Dad first, or if he reaches for her first. It looks like they both think of it at the same time. Mrs. Sidelinger pats his back over and over.

I wait until the blue minivan is gone down the road for a while before I go back to the house. I try the light switch once, then a few more times, but nothing happens. Dad pokes his head out of the kitchen.

"The power is still out. I had a visitor from down the road. A Mrs. Sidelinger. She said a big oak pulled down the lines past her house and she was letting the neighbors know. The power company is working on it now."

I join Dad in the kitchen. He's stirring something in a pot on the stove.

"Did she say anything else?"

"She mentioned they're working to restore electricity to our road by morning." Dad takes the sugar bowl off the shelf, adds a spoonful, and keeps stirring. "And she shared a bit about her own life. She is a person of great courage."

I'm glad Mrs. Sidelinger didn't say I'd been to her house.

"Dad?"

"Yes?"

"I think *you're* also a person of great courage."

"Thank you, Harvard. I'm not sure that's true, but thank you for saying it."

"What are you making?" I ask.

"Vanilla pudding. With the rest of the milk. I figure I'll use up whatever would go bad before tomorrow. If the power is still out in the morning, we can get ice."

That doesn't sound very appetizing. *What's for supper? Whatever would go bad before tomorrow.* But I do like home-made vanilla pudding.

"When I was your age," Dad says, "we had a big ice storm and lost power for two weeks. Everything froze solid and I could ride my bike through the woods on top of the ice. That was going to be Roger's next bedtime story. Maybe you'd like to hear it?"

Dad opens the refrigerator and looks in it like he's trying to decide which foods would rot the fastest.

"I'm ten. I don't need a bedtime story," I say, "but sure, maybe you can tell me about it when we're having our almost-gone-bad supper. Do you need help cooking?"

"I'm doing fine, thanks. Have you checked on the ants

lately? Some big changes, or should I say *metamorphoses*, happening."

Between Mom and Roger leaving, the bomb cyclone, the trees falling, losing power, and searching for treasure all in one day, I'd forgotten to think about the ants and how they were doing.

There are no more tiny eggs in the tunnel, and the larvae are getting bigger. For the first time, I notice that some of the larvae have turned into pupae. The cocoons look like whitish-yellow tissue paper pellets. Tenna and the workers are moving the pupae around like they're trying to figure out the best place to put them all.

I call to Dad. "We have our first pupae! They're not moving like the larvae. What do you think they're doing inside their cocoons?"

"Waiting. That's all they can do. Waiting for the next step. To become a new ant."

"Yeah, well I hope they're resting up. Because once they hatch they're going to spend the rest of their lives working."

"That's not necessarily a bad thing," he says.

While Dad cooks, I stretch out on the couch and leaf through the book Mom gave me. *Woods and Trees of Maine.* The pine tree on the cover is a white pine and it's the official Maine state tree. Its Latin name is *Pinus strobus.* There are three pages about the sugar maple, which also has a Latin name. *Acer saccharum.* There are photographs and facts about how tall it grows and what colors its leaves turn, but it's the last paragraph, and especially the last sentence, that makes me sit up.

Birdseye (sometimes written as bird's eye) maple is a
rare and mysterious feature found in few sugar maples.
Only about one percent of all maple trees contain it. No
scientific evidence is known about how it is formed, but the
one-of-a-kind wood is highly sought after by craftsmen
and artists and commands a premium price. The term
bird's eye refers to the distinctive "eyes" resembling small
bird's eyes that develop in the tree when it is young, and to
a knowledgeable person can be seen on the outside of the
tree as fissures or dents in the bark.

I stare at the words *rare and mysterious* and *dents in the bark*, and I know I can't wait until tomorrow to show Nevaeh and Mr. Knowles what *Woods and Trees of Maine* says about these *one-of-a-kind* sugar maples.

THIRTY-THREE

Windfall

D ad says I can go to Nevaeh's and show her and Mr. Knowles the tree book after supper. While we eat, he lets me use the little bit of charge left on his phone to look up bird's eye maple. I find a picture of a tabletop with what looks like miniature eyes in the grain of the wood.

Our storm meal is actually pretty good. The oven doesn't work with the power out, but Dad makes toasted grilled cheese and tomato sandwiches (using the rest of the cheese) by lighting the burners on the gas stove with a match. Dad tells me about the ice storm they had when he was my age, and how he skated in the driveway and built a snow house.

It's strange not having Roger here, being funny and loud. The roses on the table remind me of Mom. I wonder what she and Roger are doing tonight and if he is tipping himself out of his chair at home.

"Don't get your hopes up. Those trees are very old. They could be rotten inside," Dad says before I leave.

"My hopes are already up," I say.

I run into the barn house without knocking, waving the tree book in the air, opened to the page for *Acer saccharum*. I also have Dad's cell phone with the photo of the bark. Mr. Knowles is at the table, sharpening his curved hoof knife over a piece of newspaper. Nevaeh is drawing on an envelope, but quickly turns it over when she sees me.

I set the book on the table in front of Mr. Knowles, my finger under the last paragraph.

"Look at this! I think I know what your father meant about the Don't Cut 'Em trees. Right here. Bird's eye maple. *Rare and mysterious*," I quote. "And I found a photo of what the bark looks like."

Mr. Knowles reads the paragraph about bird's eye maple out loud and looks at the picture on Dad's phone.

"You know, you might be onto something, Harvard. My father was a woodworker. He built this barn and made bowls out of burls for a hobby. Who knows why he didn't say it outright, but he'd have been the person to suspect the trees had bird's eye grain in them."

"Yeah, and did you notice this?" Nevaeh has the tree book. "*Birdseye* and *bird's eye*. A word that's one word *and* two words."

"Okay, that's it," I say. "I'm making all words that way. Like *windfirm* and *wind firm*."

Mr. Knowles gets up from the table.

"Let's do it. Let's go find out."

"Now?" I ask.

"Why not? I'll get an axe and slice some of the bark off and we'll see what we see. You coming, Nevaeh?"

"Nah, too tired," she says.

"Are you sure?" I ask.

"Yeah."

That's how I end up following Mr. Knowles to the barn part of the barn house for him to get his axe and then out to one of the fallen trees.

"This looks like the photo of the bark on Dad's phone," I say, pointing to the dimpled places.

"Moment of truth," Mr. Knowles says before he raises the axe. It takes swing after swing and slice after slice to cut into the thick old bark, but when it's peeled off there are hundreds of tiny eyes in the wood.

Mr. Knowles clasps his hands together, then shakes them in front of himself and looks up into the sky.

"Thank you for looking out for me, Dad," he says. "You know what this is, Harvard? A windfall. It's truly a windfall."

"How much money do you think they're worth?" I ask.

"I don't know. I'd have to get someone in the woods business out here and have them take a look. Someone who buys high-end wood. But we've got the proof right here, don't we, all the eyes looking us right in the eye!"

"Yes! So if you sold the trees, you'd have enough money to pay off Earlene's bills, get new inhalers with all the numbers for Nevaeh, *and* buy the hay for Joker."

Mr. Knowles looks at me like I spoke in a different language.

"What do you mean, new inhalers *with all the numbers?*"

I have a good reason to speak, so I go ahead.

"Nevaeh's orange inhaler has three zeroes and the red inhaler has one zero. Except she forgot the red inhaler in your truck, so that one's gone. She told me the orange inhaler costs as much as a hundred bales of hay, enough to keep Joker fed for the winter. She thinks there might still be some medicine left in them. But Mom has asthma, too, and she said that's not how it works. Zero is really zero."

Mr. Knowles sits down on the tree and rubs his forehead. It's already a lot darker out than when we came into the woods.

"The coughing. The tiredness. Earlene would have been right on top of things. I guess I messed up. The one job that mattered."

"You didn't mess up. You're a great dad. You tell jokes and you're funny and you laugh a lot. You take Nevaeh on jobs with you. And you weren't afraid to jump in the kettle hole pond."

Mr. Knowles pushes himself off the tree like he weighs a thousand pounds.

"Thank you. You're a good friend to my daughter," he says.

When we get to the barn house, Nevaeh is asleep at the table, her head on her drawing. She's making soft snoring noises that remind me of Roger.

"Can I keep your tree book for a bit?" Mr. Knowles whispers.

"Sure, and when Nevaeh wakes up, can you tell her there's a lot of pupae in the ant farm?"

"Pupae in the ant farm. Sure. I won't forget."

Walking back, I use Dad's phone to light my way along the path and repeat the word Mr. Knowles said about the wood. "Windfall. Wind fall. Windfall. Wind fall."

THIRTY-FOUR

The Secret Word

The power comes back on the next day, and it gets hot and still, like the wind blew itself out in the storm. The tops of the trees don't move. Day after day it doesn't rain, and the lawn turns yellow in patches. *The Natural Genius of Ants* says warm temperatures speed up the development of egg to adult, and I believe it. More and more larvae turn into cocooned pupae. Tenna and her workers walk over the piles of larvae and pupae, picking them up and moving them around.

Two men come with chainsaws and a vehicle Dad calls a cable skidder. It has tires taller than me. Dad explains that they're cutting the sugar maples into lengths and stacking them by the road for a log truck to take to the sawmill.

Since Mom's visit I haven't woken up during the night. I take photos of the ant farm with Dad's phone and send them to Roger. When I call home Roger asks the same question I did.

"What are they doing inside their cocoons?"

"They're waiting. Waiting to hatch."

"Don't they get hungry in there?"

"Pupae don't need to eat."

"I'm going to ask Mom to zip me in my sleeping bag to-night, but I'm taking food in with me. In case I get hungry."

"Don't take too much food in there, or you'll end up with your own colony of ants."

"Yes!" Roger says, and hangs up before I have a chance to say anything else.

The morning before Old Home Day, Mr. Knowles borrows Dad's car and drives off with Nevaeh. He doesn't say where he's going, but he doesn't load his farrier tools in the trunk. They're gone for hours and when they return, Dad goes out to talk to Mr. Knowles. Nevaeh carries a large bag inside the house.

"What's in there?" I ask. "Did you get a bigger fishbowl for the raffle? In case the other one overflows with guesses?"

"No. Dad took me to the clinic, and then the pharmacy, and then the medical supply store. It took a long, long time. I'll show you what I got."

Everything she takes out of the bag comes in boxes, and she opens one box after the other and puts the things on the table. Three orange inhalers, two red inhalers, and a brand-new plastic submarine. A long gray plastic thing, a small black plastic thing, and a machine with an electric cord.

"Peak flow meter, oximeter, nebulizer." She touches the pieces of plastic and the machine as she names them. "They're all mine to keep. It took so long because they had to show me and Dad how to use them."

Then she takes out two pieces of paper from the bottom of the bag.

"Guess what they all cost?" she says the way Mr. Knowles asked Mom about Earlene's bills.

I pick up each orange inhaler and look in the squares at the bottom. 124. 124. 124. On the red inhalers the numbers are 200 200.

"Five hundred bales of hay's worth?" I guess.

"Pretty good guess."

"Then how did you get them? The sawyer didn't get the trees yet, did he?"

"No, he's coming for them soon. We got signed up for state aid. Dad said for everything here, it only cost as much as a bag of horse feed."

"I thought your mom didn't like taking anything from anybody?"

"She didn't. Dad said it was okay for Mom to believe that and for him to decide to keep his promise to her. And I can think that, too, when I grow up. But since I'm a child, he gets to decide, and he decided to take the help."

I pick up the inhalers again.

"That's a lot of puffs," I say.

"I know. I have to use the orange one twice a day, even if my breathing is good."

Before she leaves, we check on the ants.

"Tomorrow is Old Home Day," Nevaeh says, looking at the pupae cocoons. Every day since the storm, we've been counting down the days. It's finally only one more day.

"See you in the morning," I say. "Don't forget to pack the fishbowl, the posters, the sheet, and the clothespins."

"And you don't forget to pack the guess papers, the rock, the jar, and pencils and pens," Nevaeh says.

"And you don't forget your word for people to guess. What was it again?" I say very casually. I keep trying to surprise her into giving up the secret word.

"Hahaha!" she answers, as usual.

THIRTY-FIVE

Old Home Day

Dad sets his phone alarm for seven a.m., but we're woken at six by the rumbling of machinery. It's a truck come to get the sugar maples. Mr. Knowles and Nevaeh are already outside, watching the big metal arm with the claw clamp around each log, lift it in the air, and set it down in the truck, one by one, until they're all loaded. The man controlling the claw sits in a seat on top of the log truck and waves when he sees me. When the truck takes off, all that's left in the woods are the stumps of the fallen trees with their swirls of tree rings and the leafy-topped branches stacked in piles.

The first thing I smell when we get out of the car at Old Home Day is barbeque chicken. Smoke rises from a row of grills. I know what I'm smelling because there's a sign hanging from a tent in front of us. It says:

Old Home Day Dinner Menu

BBQ Chicken and Bean-Hole Beans

Tossed Salad, Dinner Roll & Drink

Brownie Sundae

I sniff the air. "That smell is making me hungry already."

"It's all about the food at Old Home Day," Mr. Knowles says. "Right, Marshall?"

Dad has sunglasses on, and his shirt doesn't have a pocket for his list pad and pen. He looks around at the people gathering in front of the brick town office and under the tent set up in a field.

"Nevaeh! Harvard!" Campbell calls to us. She's wearing running shoes and shorts and carrying a water bottle. Her hair is tied in two short ponytails.

"Are you going in the footrace?" I ask her.

"Yup, later today. Wanna see where your table is? I told Mom to give you the best spot."

Our raffle table is the first one you see when you go in the tent. It's near a quilt raffle and people selling jelly and wooden birdhouses. We cover the table with the sheet and clothespin the posters to it. Put the rock on the guess papers to keep them from blowing away. Set out the jar of pencils and pens.

My poster works to bring people to the table.

READ HER MIND
GUESS THE WORD
WIN A POEM
ALL ABOUT YOU

I also scout out more customers. If I see a kid around Nevaeh's age walking around, I go over with a guess paper and a pen. They look surprised but most of them still make a guess and write down their name and phone number to put in the bowl.

It turns out the grown-ups at Old Home Day want to make guesses, too. They stand there for the longest time, trying to think of the right word. Some of them stare at Nevaeh like they're actually trying to read her mind.

Nevaeh unzips the front pouch of her backpack, takes out a red inhaler, shakes it, and takes a puff.

"What's your number?"

She passes it to me, and I read what's in the square. "One ninety-two."

"Yes!" I shout, like Roger. "I bet now you can climb as many hills as you want without even stopping."

Campbell stops by the table just as a siren goes off and Nevaeh jumps up.

"The parade is starting soon. Dad said Frontier Ben is going to be in it. Can you stay at the table while I go watch? You can see it from here, but I want to get closer."

"I'll stay, too," Campbell says, and sits in Nevaeh's chair.

Once Nevaeh is out of the tent and on the side of the road with the other people waiting for the parade to start, Campbell grabs a handful of guess papers.

"How many guesses do I get?" she asks as she takes her glasses off and cleans them with her shirt.

"I don't know. We didn't set a limit. You're the first person who asked that."

She puts her glasses back on and yanks a pen out of the jar. "Great, no limit." She starts writing furiously. "Blue, green, yellow, orange, purple, red . . ." She writes one color and her name and phone number on each paper, folds them, and stuffs them in the fishbowl. Then she starts on foods. *Yogurt. Pizza. Popcorn. Squash.* Then sports. *Basketball. Soccer. Tennis. Volleyball.*

I see Mrs. Sidelinger buying a birdhouse at the wooden

birdhouse table. Her girls are with her. She sees me and smiles, then waves before walking over to the table with the jellies.

Campbell pulls more guess papers out from under the rock and stares ahead. "Can you help me? What do you think the word is?"

"Why do you want to win so bad?"

"My mother says when a girl loses her mom, her friends are really important. I'm Nevaeh's best friend. We've known each other since we were really little. Shouldn't *I* be the one to read her mind?"

The pile of guess papers is getting low.

"I have a suggestion," I say. I lean over and whisper a word in her ear.

She writes it down just as the parade begins. There's a fire engine in front, antique cars, a float with kids dressed up in old-fashioned clothes, Mr. Willette leading Frontier Ben with ribbons tied into his mane and tail, and lots of people walking and dancing along behind.

When the parade is over and Nevaeh comes back, she's surprised how many guesses are in the bowl. We join Dad and Mr. Knowles and Mr. Willette for dinner under the food tent. Dad's shirt has a bean-hole beans stain on the collar, and the ice cream on his brownie sundae melts because people keep stopping by to say hi to him. I take that as my third good-attitude win—getting Dad to come to Old Home Day and see his old friends and neighbors.

The food is even better than it smells. Nevaeh doesn't

have the barbeque chicken on her plate, and I give her my roll. After dinner, we cheer Campbell on in the footrace. She comes in second.

"Second is good," Campbell says after the race, squirting water from her water bottle on her hair, making it even shinier. "It's my personal best. I was fourth last year. And anyway, I'm training for distance, not speed. You should both go in the race with me next year."

"Maybe I will," Nevaeh says.

I shrug. I have no idea if I'll get to go to another Old Home Day. But I think of something I meant to tell Campbell.

"Remember that question you asked me, about what ants do in winter, because you never saw ants in the snow? Well, the answer is ants go into hibernation in the winter, but it's called brumation. And the reason they don't freeze is because they have something in their bodies called glycerol that protects them." I pause for full effect. "It works like ANT-i-freeze."

"Haha! I'm really gonna need some of that glycerol this winter when I'm outside waiting for the bus." Campbell pretend-shivers.

"Me too," Nevaeh says.

I wonder what winter is like here. Are there icicles as long as hockey sticks? What does it smell like when it snows?

"Mom wants me to help her set up for the talent show. When are you going to check the guesses?" Campbell asks Nevaeh.

"Probably soon. The bowl is almost full."

"Okay, see you later," Campbell says, and walks toward the town office building.

Nevaeh and I come up with a plan. I'll take the guesses out of the fishbowl, read them to her, Nevaeh will say yes or no, and I'll throw out the wrong ones. Even in the shade under the tent, it's hot. Now that the raffle is done, I tear my poster in half for each of us to use as fans.

"Summer."

"No."

"Dragonfly."

"No."

"Kettle Hole."

"No."

"Yeah, and that's two words, not one."

"Yogurt."

"No. Who would guess *yogurt*?"

"Maine."

"No."

"Stamps."

"Stamps?"

"The man from the post office made a guess."

Mosquito. No. *Moose.* No. *Blue.* No. *Sunshine.* No. *Squash.* No. *Pajamas.* No. *Umbrella.* No. *Summer.* No. *Love.* No. *Soccer.* No. *Guess.*

"Someone's guess was *guess*?"

"Yes."

"Definitely no."

"Joker."

213

"That's it!" Nevaeh shouts.

"That's your word?" I ask.

"Yes! Whose guess was it?"

I hand the paper to Nevaeh.

"It's Campbell," she says, reading the guess paper and smiling. I fan myself and then her.

"Are you glad?"

"Yes. She's my oldest friend. And now I'm all done with the promises."

"What kind of poem are you going to write about her?"

"I don't know yet." Nevaeh tilts her head to one side and then the other, studying me, kind of the way ants look at things.

"Are you having fun today?" she asks.

"Yeah."

"It seems like maybe you're not really."

"I'm having fun," I say. "Really. Old Home Day is the best."

"So?"

It's like Nevaeh is reading *my* mind, that she knows something is bothering me.

"So, soon I'll have to go home, and what if everything is the same as it was before we came here? If Dad stays in the apartment being sad all the time. And Mom is sad because he is. What if this is the last Old Home Day I go to? Look how long it took Dad to return here. Suppose I never get to come back to Kettle Hole. I don't know what it's like here in the winter. I mean, I know it's cold, like Campbell said, but I don't know what the cold smells like, or how it sounds when you walk on a frozen lake."

She doesn't say anything, but her bird eyes study my face.

"What about you?" I say. "When I'm back home, I won't get to read any of your new poems."

"Dad says cable is coming to Kettle Hole, and we have enough money to get better internet service. So I could email you my poems."

Email poems won't be the same as reading Nevaeh's small handwriting on envelopes, but I don't say that. Nevaeh looks up at the tent above us, where little birds are flying back and forth. I recognize her expression.

"You're thinking of a poem now," I say.

"Campbell's poem," she says.

I realize it's going to be up to me to make sure I get to come back, and the best way I can think of to do that involves a trip to the kettle hole pond.

THIRTY-SIX

Paid in Full

The pupae didn't hatch by Old Home Day, but it isn't long after. When I thought about a pupa hatching, I figured it would chew a hole in its cocoon and pop out in an instant. It doesn't happen like that at all. Just the way ants move dead ants or build tunnels, it's a team effort, all of them working together until the job is done.

Somehow the workers know when the first pupa is ready to come out, because they surround it, chew on the cocoon, and drag and tear at it with their legs. Sometimes they tip it over and pull on it. I think all the pupa does is get dizzy. Finally, it's freed and lays there all scrunched up, its legs tucked under itself, the way it must have been in its cocoon. The other ants move it around, like they're saying, *C'mon, there's work to be done, and we need all the help we can get.*

A week after the first one hatches, there are five new ants and all the larvae have turned into pupae. The heat wave breaks, and it gets cooler at night.

We have two weeks left in Kettle Hole. I'm still figuring out my plan to go in the kettle hole pond when Mr. Knowles knocks on the door, waving a piece of paper in the air.

"What happened?" Dad asks.

"Paid in full, that's what happened! Who says money doesn't grow on trees, right, Marshall? Thanks for the loan of your car. I got a check for the bird's eye maple logs and went to the bank and paid off the second mortgage. This is the promissory note. It means I own the house free and clear again."

"Wonderful news, Vern!" Dad gives him a hug.

"That's great!" I say.

"Yes, and now I can pay for the new truck I looked at. Would you mind giving me and Nevaeh a ride to pick it up? I promised to take her for ice cream, to celebrate, if you have time to stop on the way there. My treat!"

That's how me and Dad, Nevaeh and Mr. Knowles end up at Cone Heaven. I order a vanilla ice cream and ask how much for a cherry on top.

When the woman behind the counter gives me my cone, she says the cherry is complimentary. Nevaeh gets a chocolate chocolate chip cone, Mr. Knowles gets one called the Everything Cone, which has three flavors and sprinkles, and this time Dad gets a small coffee ice cream cone.

"Thanks," I tell Mr. Knowles.

"Thank *you*," he says. "You should consider becoming a forester, Harvard. If it wasn't for you finding out about the bird's eye, that wood would have gone up in smoke when we burned it for firewood."

Nevaeh and I get a table by ourselves.

"So you're going to move back into your house?" I say, starting in on my cone.

"Yeah. After you and your dad leave."

"Did you write your poem for Campbell?"

"Yes, but I haven't given it to her yet. Do you want to read it?"

Nevaeh takes an envelope out of her back pocket. Some of the words are scratched out, with new words written, like she couldn't decide which was the best one.

Campbell

One day she'll know every road
in town.
Not from a map
or the inside of a car
or a plane looking down.

She'll know every turn,
which roads flood in spring
where turtles cross
and turkeys are gathering.

She'll see all twenty-three miles
with her eyes,

and feel them with her feet.
So if you see her running
along your street,
wave hello
and watch her go.

"Do you think she'll like it?" Nevaeh asks.

"I think she'll LOVE it. And it's the longest poem I've ever seen you write."

Nevaeh looks relieved.

"It's the first poem I ever *had* to write. That made it hard."

After our ice cream we drop off Nevaeh and Mr. Knowles to get their truck and head back to the house.

When we go inside, the house phone is ringing. I run to answer it.

"It's me," Roger says. "I called before, but you didn't answer."

"That's because I wasn't here."

"Oh. What are you doing RIGHT NOW?" Roger asks.

"I'm talking to you."

"What is Dad doing RIGHT NOW?"

"He's watching me talk to you."

"What are you doing TOMORROW?"

This is a new one for Roger.

"I'm going for a bike ride."

When I say that, I know I can't put it off any longer. If I want to swim in the kettle hole, I can't keep worrying about how I'm going to get out—I just have to do it.

THIRTY-SEVEN

Rope

I tell Dad I'm going for a bike ride, which is true. I don't say I packed my bathing suit in my backpack.

And right before I leave, when Dad is busy in the house, I get the coil of rope I found in the shed and hang it from my handlebars. Then I take off.

I ride my bike down and up the rolling hills and past Mrs. Sidelinger's weeping willow. It's cloudy out and a little cool. On the way there I think about the eels who swim their way back to the place they were born. I looked it up on Dad's phone, and the Sargasso Sea has brown seaweed and calm blue water, and is so clear you can see down two hundred feet.

The kettle hole pond has greenish water and I can't see any farther than my own reflection. I'm not as fearless as Mr.

Knowles and not as cautious as Dad. I change into my bathing suit, tie the rope to a pine tree, and slide my way into the pond, holding the rope in one hand.

The water is warm on top and cold underneath. It's not like my dream of being in the kettle hole, where the sun was shining and the sky was blue. The sky above me is full of clouds. I let myself sink down over my head, then surface again. The water covers me, and I feel it getting in my nose and eyes and ears. That's exactly what I want. No one understands how the eels remember where to return, but I think it must have something to do with swimming in their home waters.

The clouds move fast overhead, then darken, and a light rain begins to fall. I learned to swim at the YMCA pool, and I once went in the ocean on a family vacation, but I've never been in a pond when it was raining.

I brush my wet hair off my forehead, and that's when it happens. I lose hold of the rope, and it disappears into the water as quickly as the striped snake I saw in the woods. I can see the pine tree I tied it to, but the edge of the pond is covered in grass and weeds tall enough to hide a rope.

Too late, I remember what my swim teacher taught us about the swimming buddy system.

As I paddle toward the steep edge, I try not to think about the kettle hole being bottomless. It's raining harder now, and I reach out toward the sides of the bowl-shaped pond. My fingers touch wet mud, and there's nothing to grip on to. I try again and again and again, and then I hear the slap of something hitting the water near me.

When I look over, it's the rope floating by my side, and I hear Dad's voice yelling, "Grab hold, Harvard. It's right there."

I catch the rope before it sinks again and look up at Dad. I have no idea why he's here.

I hold the rope tight in both hands, and Dad pulls from the bank.

Suddenly, he loses his footing and *splash*, we're both in the water.

"It's going to be messy, but we'll get out of here," he says. "Stay in front of me and keep hold of the rope."

We both grab the rope, and Dad pushes me ahead of him up the slippery side. My face and body press against the mud as I crawl out of the pond. Dad follows behind, pulling hand over hand with his head on my back, pushing like an ant. Finally, we make it out, both of us covered in mud.

"How did you know I was coming here?" I say when I catch my breath.

"I saw you out the window and remembered the last time *I* hung a loop of rope on *my bicycle* handlebars."

"When you helped Mr. Knowles out of the water, right? I tied it to a tree the way you did. But then I lost it."

"I saw that. You know how dangerous it is to swim alone, especially in water over your head, Harvard."

"Yes. But if Mr. Knowles's story is true, I wanted to make sure we came back to Kettle Hole again. Because I love it here and you're happy here. Or happier. You liked the ant farm and you laughed about the truck getting crushed. And you went to Old Home Day. It wasn't like when we were home. . . ."

"I know what you're saying, Harvard. These past few months have been hard for all of us."

I'm a little afraid to ask Dad the next question, but I think about it and I have a good reason.

"Will you ever be a doctor again? Because I know you're a good doctor," I say.

"I'm giving it serious thought," he says, and puts his arm around me.

Then we both get up, and Dad tips his head back so the rain falls on his face. I do the same thing, the two of us standing together, before we run down the path to the car.

Dad wrings out his shirt and pours the water out of his sneakers before he gets in. He starts the car and turns the heater on high. I don't know if it's the shock of losing the rope and thinking I might never get out of the pond, but suddenly I realize the solution to the equation Mom gave me. There's more than one answer to X. If Y is Kettle Hole, X is Roger, the ant farm, Tenna, Mom, Mr. Knowles, Nevaeh, Mrs. Sidelinger, and even me.

THIRTY-EIGHT

House Ants

The last week of summer goes by fast. I keep checking the mailbox, and there's never any mail for me until one day there is. The name and return address are McKenzie's. I open it upstairs in my room. There's a card with butterflies on the front and inside is written:

Dear Harvard,

Your father raised a very thoughtful child. We are having a baby boy next year and I hope he's as kind as you are.

McKenzie

McKenzie drew a small heart after her name. I wonder what they'll name their new baby and if he'll have as much hair as Hope. I don't need a BEEP BEEP warning to know not to show it to Dad. I put the card and envelope in the bottom of the suitcase I'm packing.

The day before we go home, Nevaeh comes over.

"Dad says you're leaving early tomorrow morning, so I should say goodbye today."

"I'll be back."

"I know. You swam in the kettle hole."

"And waded in the kettle hole mud, too! Guess what? Dad says we can all come visit in the winter when the lakes freeze."

"You mean, when *I* make the lakes freeze," she jokes.

"The ants," I say, "they're all hatched, but I don't think we should keep them in the ant farm anymore. And Dad agrees with me."

"Me neither. What are you thinking?"

"Hemlock grove!" we both say at the same time.

Nevaeh leads the way and I hug the ant farm to my chest. We walk slowly so we don't disturb the ants too much. When we get to the shady woods, I set the ant farm down near where I found the bark. Two hemlock trees are blown over, their whole root systems up in the air, facing northwest.

I don't ask her, and Nevaeh doesn't ask me, but we both know her careful hands that got the ants in the farm in the first place are the best ones to set them free.

She takes the top off, then gently slides one glass side up and out. At first, the ants don't realize there's nothing between them and the outside world. Nevaeh and I sit close by and wait. I have an idea how it will happen, because I've seen it before in the ant farm. One ant figures something out and then tells the others.

"So, Dad asked about Joker," Nevaeh says as we watch the ants.

"And?"

"He's already promised to another family for the winter."

"That's too bad."

"I know, but then Ava called Dad and said she thought I was good around horses and asked if I want to work at Second Chances Horse Haven, helping her and her wife with feeding and grooming and mucking out. And Dad said I could."

"Just watch out for Zellie!"

"I will."

Nevaeh takes a folded envelope out of her pocket.

"This is for you," she says, and watches as I unfold it.

It's a drawing of me sitting on a sugar maple log. You can see the ridges and dents in the bark. Underneath the drawing there's a poem.

Friendship
Friend ship
One word or two?
It's up to you.

"I'll hang it in my room at home," I say.

The first ant walks out of the ant farm. A second follows.

They're gone in the dirt and under the hemlock cones. Tenna is one of the last to leave. Once she's out of the ant farm, she gets up on her back legs, like she's sensing the real air and smelling the big world around her. She turns her body toward us and rotates her antenna in what looks like an ant wave, then disappears as fast as the others.

"Have a good rest of your life, Tenna," Nevaeh says.

The last morning in Kettle Hole, while Dad starts the car, I leave *The Natural Genius of Ants* book for Nevaeh on the desk. I look around to say goodbye to the house ants, but they're nowhere to be seen. Not on the floor, not on the ceiling, and not coming in or out of the cracks.

"Bye, ants, I'm leaving," I holler, in case they can hear me.

None appear anywhere, but I guess it's okay, because they were there when I needed them.

Acknowledgments

A huge thank-you to my agent, Steven Chudney, who believed I could and who continues to believe I can. I am grateful to be part of the Chudney Agency.

To my editor, Phoebe Yeh, for your insight, vision, and kindness. It has been so wonderful working with you on another book.

With appreciation for the whole team at Crown Books for Young Readers, including copyeditor Melinda Ackell, interior designer Andrea Lau, and cover designer Michelle Cunningham. Special thanks to associate editor Elizabeth Stranahan for your help and guidance.

Thank you to the Brave Union team of Kevin and Kristen Howdeshell for the inspired cover art.

With gratitude to early readers Vickie Limberger, Sylvane Pontin, Ray Pontin, Rachel Culley, Ann Dorney, and David Axelman for your time and helpful feedback.

Thank you to critique group writer friends Cathy McKelway, Sally Stanton, and Melanie Ellsworth, for reading these pages and listening to me muse about all things ant.

ABOUT THE AUTHOR

Betty Culley is the acclaimed author of the middle-grade novel *Down to Earth*, which received a starred review from *Booklist*, calling it "captivating," and the YA novel in verse *Three Things I Know Are True*, which was a Kids' Indie Next List Top Ten Pick and an ALA-YALSA Best Fiction for Young Adults nominee.

When writing *The Natural Genius of Ants*, Betty kept an ant farm and cared for a carpenter ant queen.

She's worked as a pediatric nurse and lives in a small town in central Maine.

bettyculley.com

When a huge stone falls from
the sky and lands in Henry's
backyard, that's only the start
of the adventure. . . .

"The perfect match for middle graders starting to sort
through what we do know, what we don't know yet, and
what might be unknowable."—*The Bulletin*

Available now!